Boss Me Sweetly

Boss Me, Volume 2

Cameron Hart

Published by Cameron Hart, 2023.

BOSS ME SWEETLY

First edition. September 12, 2023.

Copyright © 2023 Cameron Hart.

ISBN: 979-8227420749

Written by Cameron Hart.

Want a free book?

Sign up for my newsletter[1] and get your free copy of Chasing Stacy!

One look at the stunning waitress carrying the weight of the world on her shoulders, and I'm a goner. I wasn't looking for a sweet little thing with auburn hair and more baggage than I can fit on the back of my bike, but there's no going back now. She's mine. I'll prove to her I'm more than capable of handling her past and making her feel safe again.

1. https://dl.bookfunnel.com/7wbqvhsx8r

Connect with me!

Check out my website, cameronhart.net[2], for sneak previews on my latest projects.

Follow me on social media:

Facebook Page - facebook.com/cameronhartauthor
Instagram - instagram.com/cameron.hart.author
TikTok - tiktok.com/@author.cameron.hart
Goodreads - goodreads.com/16081533.Cameron_Hart
Bookbub - bookbub.com/authors/cameron-hart

---

2. https://cameronhart.net/

Chapter 1

Sienna

"One...more...daisy...yes! Perfection." I stand back and admire my work, wiping the thin layer of sweat off my brow with the back of my hand.

This is by far the girliest, glitteriest, over-the-top cake I've ever made. I love it. The bride asked for pink glitter marshmallow fondant, and though I've never made that, or even heard of it, I was up for the challenge. She also wanted wildflowers in every size and color spiraling down the three-tiered cake. Teal, purple, yellow, orange, blue, and of course, plenty of pink. The cake itself is strawberry flavored, with an orange creamsicle filling. Again, not a combination I've ever heard of, but damn if it isn't delicious.

I've made some pretty incredible masterpieces in the short time I've owned this bakery if I do say so myself, but this one is in a completely different league. It's not something I ever would have come up with on my own, but after talking with the bubbly and bright Luna Foster, soon to be Luna Knight, we designed the perfect cake for her wedding.

While I enjoy the day-to-day baking tasks that keep this little bakery open, these custom orders are what I live for. I've poured my heart and soul into this cake, and today is the big day. I take a few more pictures of the most gorgeous cake I've ever made and make a note to ask Luna if I can get a photo of when the two of them cut the cake.

Looking at the clock, I go into panic mode. I should have left ten minutes ago, but I got caught up in decorating and daydreaming. Fuck. I wanted to change my clothes and look a little more presentable in case I run into anyone at the wedding who might want my business card. As it is, I'll have to go in what I'm wearing – yoga pants, a baggy sweatshirt, and scuffed-up Vans. Very professional.

No time to worry about that now. I wash my hands and package the cake up, getting it ready to transport. This is only my second delivery, and while my one and only part-time worker, Mandy, offered to do it, I insisted on hand-delivering this one myself. If I'm honest, I don't trust anyone else to handle this cake. I need to be the one to carry it into the reception hall and set it down on the table to ensure it made it there in one piece and nothing goes wrong. Does that make me a bit of a control freak? Probably. So be it.

After securing the cake in my car with the help of Mandy, I type out location of the reception on my phone and pull into traffic. Other cars honk at me for going five below the speed limit, and I dutifully honk right back, giving them the middle finger for good measure. Some might call it road rage, but I call it being a New Yorker. Granted, I've only been one for the last year, but I like to think I've adapted to my surroundings quite well.

On top of the late start from my shop in Brooklyn to the reception hall in Tribeca, there's an accident on the Brooklyn Bridge, because of course there is.

"Fuck," I hiss out, staring at the clock on my dashboard.

It figures. The most gorgeous cake I've ever made, for the fancy wedding of a billionaire, and I'm going to screw it up by being late.

Do you really think you can make it on your own? You're going to screw everything up and come crawling back to me, you ungrateful bitch.

I've been gone for over a year, but her voice seems to be stuck in my head. Nails on a chalkboard. More like used needles on a chipped Formica countertop. I lay on the horn trying to drown out the voice in my head.

Twenty agonizing minutes later, I pull off the bridge and speed as carefully as I can, to the reception hall. I know it's already started; I just hope they have a seven-course meal or whatever it is rich people do for weddings.

Parking by the back entrance, I set up my little cart and place the cake just so, somehow managing to get it out of the backseat on my own. I maneuver the cart up the ramp and prop the door open, wheeling the cake and cart into the kitchen. Peering into the reception hall, I breathe a sigh of relief to see the guests are still working on their steak dinner.

I turn back to my cart and begin walking backward, pulling the cart along as my butt pushes open the swinging door. The wheel gets stuck on the lip of the door frame, so I tug gently at the cart, cursing whoever installed the door. The cart doesn't give at all, so I push it forward, repositioning the wheel, and try tugging again. And again. And again.

My foot slips from underneath me, the traction in my old sneakers long worn down. I feel myself falling backward in slow motion while the cart finally pops free from the door frame and threatens to roll right over me. Fan-fucking-tastic. Not only am I going to ruin the sweet Luna's wedding, but I'm going to make a gigantic fool out of myself in the process.

Instead of falling to my untimely and embarrassing demise, I feel a strong hand steady me between my shoulder blades while another hand reaches in front of me to stop the cart. I gasp in surprise and hold my breath while squeezing my eyes shut, waiting for the cake to topple over or my knees to give out. Neither of those things happen.

"Are you okay?" The smooth, deep voice of my savior causes me to open my eyes and take a breath. It also causes my heart to stutter in my chest for some reason.

Slowly, I turn around and stare up into the bluest eyes I've ever seen. They are full of concern and kindness. I don't think anyone has looked at me that way other than my Grams, and certainly not drop-dead gorgeous men like this one. He's seriously stunning.

Styled yet perfectly messy brown hair, thick eyebrows, and long lashes I'd kill for, framing his crystal blue eyes. He's got a sharp nose, soft lips, and strong jaw, each feature perfectly complimenting the others. He even has a few tattoos poking out from the collar of his dress shirt, which completes the sexy, bad boy with a heart of gold package. Then he smiles at me.

And now my knees actually do give out.

My handsome savior pulls me into his large body with a hand on the small of my back. All the air drains from my lungs when I feel his hard muscles press up against my soft curves. I still can't take my eyes off his, like he's holding me hostage.

"Careful there, sweetness," he murmurs.

Just like that, the spell is broken.

"I'm no one's *sweetness*," I snap, trying to wriggle out of his hold.

Instead of letting me go, he chuckles. The warm, gravelly sound washes over me and makes me ache in totally inappropriate places. My gorgeous savior turned captor lifts a hand up to my face and swipes his thumb over my right eyebrow. I narrow my eyes at him, but then he pulls his thumb away, showing me a streak of frosting he wiped off.

Looking me square in the eyes, he brings the frosting to his lips and sucks it off the pad of his finger, groaning at the taste.

Oh shit, my panties are wet. What the actual fuck is wrong with me?

He grins down at me, showing off his white teeth and a devious sparkle in his eyes. "Delicious, just like I thought, sweetness."

I do my best to scowl at him, despite the heat coursing through my body and pooling between my thighs. I do *not* need this arrogant asshole hitting on me during the biggest delivery of my short career as a baker. I jerk away from his embrace, and this time, he lets me go.

Continuing on my mission to get the cake set up, I push the cart over to the table and come up with a game plan for transferring the monstrosity.

"Need some help?" The handsome jerk asks, that huge smile still on his face. The guy has dimples, because of course he does. It's not even fair.

"No, I'm fine, thanks. Go back to your steak dinner," I say in my coldest tone, waving him off.

"Maybe you were right. Not so sweet after all, huh? More like...a kitten. Adorable with sharp claws."

"Is that what it would take to get you to fuck off? Clawing you?"

His eyes turn dark, which doesn't help my confusing state of arousal.

"I don't know, maybe you should try," he responds, smirking like the asshole he is. The sexy, impossible to ignore asshole who is making me feel...*things*.

I turn my back to him and scoot the cart up close to the table. I have no idea how I got this behemoth of a cake out of my Jeep without the help of Mandy, but if I did that, I can do this. Except now my hands are sweaty and I have an audience.

I tilt my head back and stare at the ceiling, taking a deep, controlled breath. When I look back down, I notice the gorgeous jerk has moved around to face me again. He's smirking and waiting for me to ask for his help.

The man quirks an eyebrow up in challenge, which makes me grit my teeth. I don't know what it is about this guy, but I want to push him away and pull him close and tell him to go to hell and also tell him to never leave me.

I mean, who is this guy? He's trouble, that's what he is. A distraction. A beautiful, tall, blue-eyed distraction, but that's no matter. He's the opposite of what I need right now. I'm just trying to lay low. Start over. Gain some footing and confidence.

I clear my throat and disperse any and all thoughts of the man-candy standing far too close to me. Slipping my hands under the cake, I prepare to lift and ease it onto the table. It's surprisingly easy and the whole thing is done in about ten seconds.

Ha. Take that, Mr. Too-Handsome-For-His-Own-Good.

And then I his hands slide out from under the cake stand, letting me know he helped me after all.

"I could have done it myself. I don't need your help," I mutter. "Not every woman is looking for a knight in shining armor, you know."

"Ah, I suppose it's just in my nature, then. I didn't mean to offend your sensibilities." He grins at me, the bastard.

"My *sensibilities*?! Who do you think you are?"

He holds out his hand, and I can't help but notice tattoos peeking out of his sleeve. The guy must be covered in them, and I won't lie, I want to see them all.

"I'm Cooper Knight. My shining armor is at the cleaners, so this tux had to do."

"You've got to be fucking kidding me," I grumble. I know I should backtrack, try to save face. However, apologies aren't really my thing. Neither is being fake nice to get what I want.

Cooper smiles that big, stupid, sexy smile and takes my hand in his for a handshake. I swear to God, my hand tingles and something spikes my heartrate when his large hand engulfs my much smaller one. It's cheesy as fuck and I wouldn't believe it if it weren't happening to me right now.

I try pulling my hand away, but Cooper tightens his grip and tugs me into his hard, warm body once again. I hate how his cinnamon and spice smell invades my senses and how his breathing anchors me. I hate how his eyes peer down into mine and make me feel seen for the first time in so long. I really hate the protective way he holds me, like his place is now between me and the rest of the world. Wouldn't that be nice? Too bad life doesn't work like that.

"I know you feel it too," he whispers.

"I don't feel anything," I lie. Am I trembling in his arms right now? Why can't I breathe? What is happening to my stupid heart that's making it pound violently in my chest?

Cooper grins at me, that dimple popping out, those blue eyes twinkling. He cups the side of my face, and despite my brain screaming for me to run away, I lean into his touch. God, how long has it been since someone has been this close to me? Treated me so tenderly? Am I really so lonely and starved for human connection?

"You're lying, kitten," he whispers. Cooper looks at me with such intensity and longing. No one has ever looked at me that way. It's too much. But I'm frozen in place, waiting for his next move. "You're scared," he says more to himself than to me.

I don't like that he can read me so easily. I *really* don't like that he slipped right under all my defenses and rendered me speechless, practically melting in his strong embrace. My survival instincts finally kick in, and I do the only thing I can think of to get him to back the fuck off.

I slap him. Hard.

He instantly releases me, and I recoil on instinct, waiting for his anger, his retaliation. Instead, Cooper grins, even as he's rubbing his cheek. I grab my cart and high tail it out of there. The farther away I get from Cooper, the more my heart and mind battle each other. I want him. I hate him. He feels safe. He could break me. He feels like home. I could never belong in his world.

Don't look back, don't look back, don't you dare look back.

I look back.

Cooper is standing there smiling at me in equal parts disbelief and awe. My heart flutters while other parts of me throb. I growl at myself for being weak.

Back in my car, I take a few cleansing breaths. I open my eyes and stare at myself in the rearview mirror. "Get ahold of yourself. You're stronger than this. You don't need no man, especially that arrogant jerk. You'll never see him again anyway, so it doesn't matter."

I shove down the sinking feeling in my stomach at the thought of never seeing Cooper again. I'm sure I'll forget all about him by the end of the day, just like he'll forget about me.

Chapter 2

Cooper

My cheek stings from where my little kitten slapped me, but I can't stop the grin that spreads across my face. She's mine. I know it. I fucking feel it. I know she feels it too, especially when she looks at me over her shoulder, those hazel eyes searching me, fighting me, surrendering to me. She scowls, which only makes me want her more.

Clad in yoga pants, an old baggy sweatshirt, ratty sneakers, and a mess of black hair piled on top of her head, I've never seen anyone as beautiful as my sweetness. I don't even know her name, but I will.

"What's going on with you?" My brother, Declan, asks.

"I just met my future wife," I tell him, still looking at the door my kitten just went through.

"Really?!" Luna says excitedly. "How romantic! Who is she?"

"I have no fucking clue."

Declan claps me on the shoulder and gives me a knowing look. He and his new bride had a rocky start, but they are so in love it's ridiculous. Even more shocking is the fact that my stubborn, hardass brother is a freaking teddy bear when it comes to Luna, though it took some time for him to come around to the idea of love.

Not me. I had my fill of empty relationships, and now I'm ready for something real. Something life-altering. Something like my sweet little baker with the chip on her shoulder. She's probably a good ten years younger than my thirty-one, which brings out this protective instinct in me. She's all fire and fury, but underneath all of that, I see her. The real her. I tore her wide open just like she did me. She felt vulnerable and threatened, but I'll show her she has nothing to fear from me. I'll only ever love her and protect her. Whoever she is.

Which reminds me, I need to ask Luna where she got the cake. But...not right now. She's currently being cutesy with Declan, which is still such a strange sight. I'm happy for him, though. Hopefully one day soon it will be my kitten and me getting married and rubbing frosting on each other's faces. And other places.

Well, damn. Now all I can think about is trailing frosting down my woman's sexy little body and licking it up, inch by inch.

I clear my throat and get my hardening cock under control. This is neither the time nor the place to be having such thoughts.

Soon, sweetness. Soon you'll be mine like I'm already yours.

***

Luna and Declan just got back from their honeymoon, thank *God*. It's taken every bit of self-control I have not to bother them while they are away. But their flight landed an hour ago, which means I'm already an hour behind schedule to finding out who my future wife is.

It should shock me how much I'm already consumed by her, but it doesn't. Like I said, I've been ready for the right woman to come along. I knew the next time I was with in a relationship with someone, they would be my forever.

I was infatuated with my feisty little kitten from the moment she fell into my arms, and I expected to obsess over her in the days leading up to finding her again. But I wasn't prepared for the ache of being separated. This last week I kept replaying our short time together. The way she felt in my arms, so tiny and perfect. The cute little smudge of frosting over her eyebrow. The white, creamy skin dotted with freckles on her nose and cheeks. I want to taste each one. And her eyes. Goddamn. Brown at the center that fades to green and then blue, complete with golden flecks. I can't get them out of my head.

When I touched her hand, my whole body lit up. I can't explain it, and I won't even try to understand it, but it only confirmed what I already knew; this woman isn't like anyone I've ever met.

Then she went and slapped the fuck out of me, as if I needed another reason to keep her around forever. I won't lie, that had me sporting a semi for a long time after she left. I'm going to enjoy getting under her skin and winding my way into her life and her heart. God knows she's already the center of my world and I don't even know her name.

My phone rings, flashing Declan's name across the screen. Thank fuck.

"Bro—"

"Is everything okay? I have ten missed calls from you," Declan gets out all in a rush.

"Yeah, well, no, but not like what you're thinking."

"Out with it."

"I need the name of the baker and bakery you got your cake from."

There's a pause.

"Seriously?" He growls.

"Yes."

More silence. Then I hear muffled voices, one of which belongs to Luna.

"Luna says the cake was from Mad Batter Bakery, owned by Sienna Carmichael."

"Sienna," I say to myself. I curl her name around in my head, on my tongue, deep in my throat, all the way down in my chest. It punctures my lungs and becomes the very air I breathe.

"What is this about, then? What's the big deal?" Declan sounds annoyed, but fuck if I care. My world is currently being turned upside down once again with the knowledge of being *that* much closer to my kitten.

"Declan!" Luna chastises him. It brings me back to the present and makes me snicker at the thought of the tiny little Luna putting Declan in his place. "Leave Cooper alone. He's in love with Sienna, leave the man be!"

Declan grunts and I hear Luna giggle. "That true, Coop?" He asks.

"Yup. She's going to be my wife."

"Well, damn. That happened kinda quick, don't you think?"

"Not at all. I've been going out of my goddamn mind waiting for you guys to get back from your honeymoon so I could find out who Sienna is. A week is too long to be away from her."

"Listen, brother, I'm happy for you. Truly, I am. But I think you need to dial back the intensity. You're going to scare the poor girl away."

I sigh. "You're probably right. But I can't help it."

"Don't whine. And don't be a creep."

"Any other sage advice?" I joke.

"Don't give up on her!" Luna shouts. "And be genuine. She can spot a fake from a mile away."

"Got it. Thanks, Luna."

"I'm hanging up now, Cooper. Don't bother me again for at least forty-eight hours. The honeymoon isn't over yet."

"Declan! Oh my god!" Luna squeals. I chuckle, knowing she's probably blushing right about now.

I put my phone down and take a deep breath, trying to compose myself. Declan is right. I'm going to come on too strong and scare her away.

In an attempt to slow down and not rush over to her right this damn second and kiss her soft, pink lips, I look up Mad Batter Bakery. There's surprisingly little information available about the shop. No website, only the bare minimum listed on Google. I do, however, see that there's an Instagram for Mad Batter Bakery.

Clicking over to that, I start scrolling through the photos. Each one is incredible. Cookies meticulously decorated with lace trim, mouth-watering cupcakes, decadent cakes with intricate swirls of frosting. She's truly incredible. How has she flown under the radar? Her designs, unique recipes, and the location in Brooklyn should all make for a wildly successful business. And yet, from what I can tell, she's making enough to keep the lights on and not much more.

Good thing I'm co-CEO of White Knight Advertising. I think I just found my next client. Not that I'd charge her for my services, of course.

I look at my watch and see it's almost three in the afternoon. It's been a whole thirty minutes since I've gotten Sienna's name and information and I haven't knocked down her door yet, which I think shows an immense amount of self-control.

But I can't wait any longer.

I hop in my Lamborghini, the one ridiculous thing I own aside from my penthouse. My brothers, Declan and Asher, like to use a driver, but not me. It's not so much the flashiness of the car – I mean, hell, if I really wanted to impress people, I could have gotten a Bugatti, but I always wanted a Lambo. Even more so since my dad said it was impractical and immature.

When the old man passed away last year, we all handled it differently. Asher became even more cold and distant, which is saying something. Declan seemed all keyed up on proving dad wrong and got lost in his head for a while until Luna came along.

To be fair, our father was an asshole. The man was manipulative, always gave backhanded compliments, and pitted us against each other mercilessly. When he died, all I felt was freedom. Declan, Asher, and I didn't have to fight anymore, we didn't have to do what he said, didn't have to perform. So, I got the car I always wanted and took it on a nice long drive the day after his funeral.

My phone barks at me, letting me know my destination is on my right. Sure enough, Mad Batter Bakery comes into view. Damn, the place even has parking. How did Sienna get this little gem of a location? And why isn't her business blowing up? I guess I'll find out soon.

Walking in the front door of the little shop, I take note of the bold way it is decorated. The floor is a classic black and white checker, the walls exposed brick. The décor is colorful and eclectic, including some callbacks to Alice in Wonderland. The tables and chairs are all mismatched but in an intentional way. Each table has a teapot and a stack of mismatched teacups. It's out there but in the best way possible. Fun and quirky and perfectly marketable. Why hasn't she done more to drum up business?

I finally get to the counter, where I'm greeted by someone who isn't my Sienna.

"Hi, welcome to Mad Batter Bakery. What can I get for you?" The woman behind the counter asks. She's smiling a little too much as her eyes rake up and down my body. I've seen that look before. Hard pass. Now that I've seen my kitten and held her in my arms, no one else will ever come close.

"I'm actually looking for—"

I'm cut off by a loud crash from the back of the shop. I look over to the source of the commotion and see the woman of my dreams staring wide-eyed at me.

"You…" She squeaks out.

While Sienna comes to terms with the fact that I found her, I take a second to look her over again. Her hair is up in another messy bun and she has flour on her cheek. She also has a sleeve of tattoos that I didn't see before since she was wearing a sweatshirt. Fuck that's hot. I want to trace her ink and make her tell me the story behind every tattoo she has.

"Me," I finally answer her with a smile.

"What…how…why?" She's freaking adorable all flustered and blushing. Sienna shakes her head as if trying to dispel her nerves and come up with a way to kick me out of her bakery. I welcome the challenge.

She clears her throat and tries again. "Cooper. What are you doing here?" My little kitten is trying to be cold, but the fact that she remembers my name shows that she's been thinking about me too.

"I'm here to see you, of course." *Damn, reel it in.* "I was thinking, I could offer my services."

She rolls her eyes dramatically and bends over to clean up the metal bowl she dropped. Fuck, she's so effortlessly sexy in her tank top and yoga pants. "Funny, I was thinking we've already gone over this. I don't need or want your help," she fires back.

"Ah, but didn't I prove myself useful before, even when you were refusing me?"

Instead of answering, Sienna grabs a broom and starts sweeping up the spilled flour on the floor. I glance over at the girl who greeted me and see she's busy helping another customer, giving me the perfect opportunity to slip behind the counter.

When my kitten looks up, she seems startled to see me this close.

"You can't be back here," she bites out, pointing at me with a wooden spoon. Her words say one thing, but her body language says another. I can see her chest heaving with shallow breaths. She's trying to be angry with me, but her pupils are dilated. She likes what she sees, and that makes me want to beat my chest with pride. I can practically see her pulse racing in the side of her neck, and Jesus, do I want to kiss that spot and make her squirm.

"I just want to talk. You know I'm co-CEO of White Knight Advertising, right?"

She snorts, somehow managing to make even that adorable. "Co-CEO? Couldn't quite hack it on your own then?"

Her words hit a little too close to home, hurting more than I think she meant them too. It's okay, though. I know she's being defensive. I can take whatever she dishes out.

"My brothers and I are all CEOs. But that's beside the point. I'd like to help get this place on the map. You're quite talented and you have a great location. I can set you up with a website, a social media strategy, and kickstart ads on Google and Facebook. What do you say? Free of charge, of course."

She stares at me, though not with the gratitude I was hoping for.

"No."

"No?" I truly was not expecting that. I thought this would be my in, a way for me to work with her and spend time with her.

"That's right. Not used to hearing that word, are you? I'll say it again. No. I don't want your *services*. Thanks, but no thanks."

"Can I ask why?"

"You can, but that doesn't mean I'll answer." Her eyes flash a challenge at me, the hint of a smirk playing at those soft lips of hers.

"Fair enough," I smirk at her, letting her know I'm up for her games, whatever they may be. "Are you a native New Yorker?"

She doesn't say anything, she just turns and goes back to whatever recipe she was working on before she dropped the bowl. I watch as she measures out the dry ingredients in one bowl, sifting the flour, baking powder, and spices together. She's absolutely mesmerizing.

"Not that it's any of your business, but no," she clips out. At least she's answering me, however begrudgingly it may be.

I grin, knowing I'm getting to her just a little bit. "Not that you asked, but I was born and raised here," I say.

"Oh yeah? Silver spoon and all?"

"Well, yeah. How else would I eat my caviar?"

Sienna tries, unsuccessfully, to hide her smile. She turns the bowl over and dumps a ball of dough out on the lightly floured counter and begins kneading it. I can't help but appreciate the way her slim, toned arms flex as she folds and manipulates the dough.

"How long have you been open for business?" I ask.

She gives me the side-eye, probably picking up on my not so subtle innuendo.

"The bakery has been here for a year."

"Where did you learn to bake?"

"My grandma," she grits out after punching the dough with a little more force than necessary.

"Are you still close?"

Sienna closes her eyes and clenches her jaw, taking a deep breath. The mood has shifted, and I know I pushed too hard.

"She's dead. Is that what you want to hear?" She snaps, her hands going to her hips as she turns around and glares at me.

My stomach clenches at the thought of her experiencing any kind of loss.

"No, of course not, I'm sorry—"

"What's all this about, anyway? I told you I don't want your help or your pity service or whatever. Why are you still here?"

"It's not pity. I'm just trying to get to know you—"

"I don't want to be known. Please leave."

Well, fuck. This is not going how I planned at all. What does she mean she doesn't want to be known? Too damn bad, she's mine and I'm going to dismantle her defenses and get all of her secrets. I'll know every single thing about her, what makes her laugh, what makes her cry, what makes her scream in pleasure.

There's no hiding from me, sweetness, and when you're ready, I'll show you what it means to be loved like you deserve.

"I'm sorry if I made you uncomfortable, Sienna."

Her face turns deathly white and she backs into the counter, gripping the edges to hold herself up. I step towards her, hating the way she's cowering in fear over something I said. She flinches, which makes my chest nearly cave in. I just want to comfort her, but something I did made her this way.

"How do you know my name?" She whispers.

"I asked my sister-in-law who you made the beautiful wedding cake for. You remember Luna?" I say in the most calming voice I can muster. I want to hold her and ask her what the fuck she's afraid of, but I know I can't do any of that right now.

"Right," she breathes out, her shoulders relaxing and her grip loosening from the counter. Sienna closes her eyes and takes another deep breath. Then, her eyes snap open and she shoots a death glare my way. "You," she spits out. "Out. Now. I knew you were trouble. I don't need trouble."

"Sienna..."

"Out. Get the fuck out of my kitchen."

"I'm sorry," I tell her. I'm at a complete loss for words and I have no idea how to get her to let me stay. I spooked her and that made her feel weak, so now she's lashing out. I get it. But I don't like it.

She doesn't say anything, just stands there with her arms crossed over her chest in a defensive stance. Her eyes are hard, and her chin is held high, but I see her trembling despite her strong front.

I back away, but not before looking into those beautiful eyes of hers. "I'd never hurt you, Sienna." I silently plead with her to trust me.

For a brief second, her walls come down, allowing her eyes to flood with conflicting emotions. I see pain and pride, defeat and determination, fear and fierceness. But then anger takes over and her walls come up once again.

In a last-ditch effort to connect with her, I reach into my pocket and get a business card. I write down my cell phone number on the back and place the card down on the counter. I try to think of something else to say, but I come up empty.

Taking a deep breath, I do the hardest thing I've ever done in my life. I walk away from Sienna. I'll be back for her, though. I just have to change up my tactic, regroup a bit. She's mine, and I protect what's mine.

Chapter 3

Sienna

I manage to finish out the day in the shop, despite being rattled to my very core. Now I'm sitting on my couch with a much-deserved glass of wine. I mean, who the hell does Cooper Knight think he is?

Oh, right. *Cooper Knight.*

He thinks he can just waltz into my bakery and turn on the charm and...and...what? Sleep with me? Is that his end goal? I won't lie, my lady parts like that thought. A lot. And sure, I *want* to believe him when he says he just wants to help and he'd never hurt me, but I know better.

I won't become my mom, always going from guy to guy, looking all wide-eyed and pathetic and crying about her problems to any man who will listen. I saw what kind of company that behavior attracted. Hell, I *lived* with that kind of company. The kind who hand out favors with strings attached. The kind who will say anything to fulfill some carnal need, and then bail the second things get too real.

That's probably why I'm still a virgin at twenty-one. I don't trust anyone, period, let alone trust someone enough to be that vulnerable. My mom taught me how to spot charismatic, manipulative bastards. I learned a hell of a lot from her mistakes. I'm hardly ever wrong when it comes to spotting a user. Then again, I don't really give people the chance to prove me wrong, but still.

Cooper Knight is definitely a bastard.

Right?

I can't tell. And that right there is a red flag.

He's arrogant, that's for sure. And charming. *Too* charming. He offered to give my bakery a nifty little marketing facelift, which I'm guessing is worth a few thousand dollars. And that's another thing. He's rich. Like, richer than anyone I've ever known. All of these signs point to someone who wants to use me and throw me away.

But then there are his eyes. The way he looks at me, *really* looks at me. And I'd be lying if I said I haven't been thinking about the way it felt to be in his arms. All week I've replayed those few moments we shared, him pulling me into his chest, touching my face so sweetly, peering into the very depths of me and refusing to back down. You can't fake that, right?

I'm sure my mom thought that dozens of times though, and each boyfriend only seemed to get worse the more desperate she got. Which is why I won't ever go down that path. I refuse to need anything from anyone. I'm fine on my own, I'm making it work. So what if I'm a little lonely? Small price to pay for being independent.

Then why have I been folding and unfolding the corner of Cooper's business card all night?

"Dammit," I curse under my breath.

I put the card on my coffee table and stare at it as if it betrayed me. I should throw it away. Really, I should. And I will. Totally will. As soon as I get up. But first I need to finish my wine. And maybe snuggle up with my fleece blanket...

"Now we let the dough rest and rise," Grams tells me.

"But why can't we use it now?"

"Ah, so impatient, Sienna. We have to give it time. You can't rush these things if you want fluffy, flakey cinnamon rolls."

"But why?"

"So full of questions lately," she smiles. "I love that about you. Always curious. We have to let the dough rest so that the yeast – that little packet we added – can react with the sugar. The yeast eats up the sugar and then releases something called carbon dioxide, which makes the dough expand."

I nod studiously, trying to make sense of her answer. Grams laughs. It's a warm sound that always makes me laugh along with her.

"That's probably way too detailed for a six-year-old," she says, shaking her head.

"It's okay. What's cardboard die oxen?" I ask.

"Car-bon di-ox-ide."

"Car-bon di-ox-ide," I repeat. "What's that?"

"How about I give you a science lesson later? I have a fun experiment we can do with Mentos and Diet Coke."

"Really?!" Baking and experimenting in one afternoon? I love coming to grandma's house.

"Really," she smiles down at me. "Now, how about we make the filling? Remember the secret ingredient?"

"Corn starch!"

"That's right!" She gives me a high five and lets me measure out the cinnamon, brown sugar, and corn starch.

"Grams, do you think we could—"

"MOTHER!" The front door swings open with a bang and my mom storms through. Her voice is angry, and her eyes are red. I hate when she gets like this.

"Angie," Grams says. "Why don't you go take a nap."

"I'm not a child anymore, mother. You can't control me."

I step in between Grams and mom. Sometimes mom can be unpredictable when she gets like this. I don't want her to hurt Grams. In fact, I don't want her here at all. She's ruining my perfect afternoon.

"Sienna, honey, why don't you go downstairs and watch tv?" Grams tells me in her calm voice. I don't want to leave her alone with mom, but I also don't want to disobey Grams. I nod and go downstairs, keeping my head down so I don't have to look at my mom.

I turn the tv on, but I still hear mom and Grams arguing about money. It's always about money.

I must have fallen asleep, because the next thing I know, mom is shaking me.

"Hey, there my beautiful baby," she coos. I don't like that voice. It's too sweet. I don't trust it.

"Mommy?"

"It's time to go. We have to be quiet, okay? We don't want to wake up Grams."

I yawn and crawl off the couch. I notice something shiny hanging out of mom's big purse. Without thinking, I reach for it.

"Pretty!" I exclaim once I have the gold necklace in my hands.

Mom slaps my hand and yanks the necklace away. The motion knocks her purse off her shoulder. Sparkly earrings, a pearl necklace, and a large diamond ring all come tumbling out of the purse when it hits the ground.

"Clumsy bitch!" Mom snaps.

"Sorry mommy, I'll help—"

"No, you've done enough," she says angrily as she stuffs the pretty jewelry back in her purse. "Let's go. Don't touch anything and don't make a noise."

"I want to say goodbye to grandma."

"No."

"But why?"

She grabs my face and digs her fingers into my cheeks. Tears form in my eyes, but I try holding them back. I know mommy hates when I cry.

"Stop asking questions. Stop talking. I told you we're leaving, so we're leaving. Understood?"

I nod as best as I can while she's holding my face. Mom lets me go and I can't hold back the whimper or sniffle that escapes.

One minute I'm standing, and the next minute I'm on the floor, the side of my face on fire from the back of my mom's hand.

I snort awake and throw the fleece blanket off of me. I must have fallen asleep on the couch. I rub my temples in an attempt to rid myself of the memory. I don't know why I go back to that one more often than not. It's certainly not the most traumatic thing my mom ever did to me, and half of that memory is actually really good. I always loved baking with my Grams. She was so patient with me and taught me the science behind each ingredient.

I wish my mom would have just left me with Grams. It was obvious to me, even at that young age, that my mom didn't want me.

You're the reason no one wants me, Sienna.

The specifics changed as I grew older. At first, I was too clingy. *No one wants to be with me because you're such a needy child.* And then it was because I was in the way. *You're always underfoot and babbling about something.* Finally, when my boobs grew in, my mom said I was a little slut who tempted her boyfriends.

Gross. The thought of any of her string of disgusting boyfriends touching me makes bile rise up in the back of my throat. Thank fuck things never went that far.

I sigh and put my head in my hands, wincing when I poke myself in the face with something.

Cooper's business card.

How the fuck did that get in my hand? Have I been holding it this whole time? What the hell? I've been clinging to the dang piece of cardstock like it's my security blanket.

I ignore the tightness in my chest when I think about being safe in Cooper's arms. I absolutely don't give into the fantasy of letting him take care of me. I definitely don't let my mind wander to what it would be like to kiss him.

Nope, not me. I don't need Cooper. Or want him.

***

It's been three days since I last saw Cooper. Not that I'm counting. Not that I care. I'm just saying. For a guy who was so insistent on helping me, he sure gave up easily enough.

Well, good. That's what I wanted, after all. Is it really surprising that he hasn't shown his face around here? I have been nothing but a total bitch to him. Of course, he would want nothing to do with me after I yelled at him and kicked him out of my shop.

Then why did he give you his business card and cell phone number?

It doesn't matter. It's not like I've called or texted him.

But you haven't thrown the card away, either.

Damn my inner monologue!

I let out a frustrated breath and get to work on frosting cookies. These frosted lace cookies were the first item to sell out when I opened the shop a year ago. By noon on my opening day, I had sold the whole batch and had requests for more. Word of mouth got around after that, and things have been pretty perfect around here with just enough work for Mandy and me and enough money to pay the bills and lay low. What more could a girl ask for?

Oh, I don't know. Super hot sex with the dark-haired, blue-eyed Greek god of a man who has been starring in your dirty dreams?

"Seriously?!"

"Everything okay?" Mandy asks from the front counter.

"Yeah, sorry. Just talking to myself."

Mandy hums something in acknowledgment and goes back to wiping down the counter. The bell on the front door rings as a customer walks in. I continue the tedious yet calming process of piping on the frosting one string of lace at a time.

"Hello again," I hear Mandy greet whoever just walked in. I know that voice. It's her *I'm sexy but in a coy way that implies I'm a lady in the streets and a freak in the sheets* voice. I roll my eyes at her failed attempt to be subtle.

"Hey," comes the reply.

Oh shit.

I know that voice.

"Two times in one week, lucky me," Mandy drawls. It shouldn't make me want to fire her, but it does. I shouldn't care if she flirts with Cooper, or if *anyone* flirts with Cooper, for that matter.

And yet...

"Is Sienna here?" Cooper asks, not falling for Mandy's schtick. I can't help but smirk a little at that. Only because Mandy is so pretty, and she never gets turned down. Yes, that's why I'm smirking. No other reason.

"In the back. Want me to—"

"I know where it is," he dismisses her.

Double shit. He's coming back here.

I don't know what to say or how to act or apparently what to do with my hands anymore. What the hell is wrong with me? Would he notice if I hid inside of the gigantic mixer? No, that would be a bitch to sanitize again today. His footsteps are getting closer, closer...

"Sienna," his rich voice washes over me. It calms me and yet somehow spikes my adrenaline.

I shove a cookie in my mouth.

Because I'm an idiot and I cannot *even* right now.

Instead of chewing the cookie, I sort of inhale it, which makes me cough.

"Hey, woah, are you alright?" Cooper is on me in a flash, rubbing my back and telling me to breathe.

God, could you be a bigger fool right now?

I cover my mouth with my hand and swallow the rest of the cookie before looking up at Cooper. At first, he looks worried, which kind of makes me melt for him. But then he gets that cocky grin on his face, making it easier to not like him.

"Sampling the goods, eh?"

"Just one of the many perks of owning your own bakery," I say, a little too proud of myself for actually responding and not spewing cookie crumbs all over his stupidly handsome face.

Cooper smiles down at me, hooking me in with those gorgeous eyes of his. He leans down ever so slightly. I should move. I really should. I think he's going to kiss me, which would be a colossal mistake on so many levels.

And yet...my lips part slightly and my head tilts up towards his. My body is rebelling against the clear command my brain is giving, which is, *slap that jerk right is his perfect face and run*!

Instead of kissing me, Cooper wipes his thumb over the corner of my mouth, collecting a bit of frosting from the earlier cookie fiasco. Embarrassment floods my cheeks, but Cooper doesn't pull his hand away. No, he presses his frosting-covered thumb in between my parted lips.

I have no choice but to lick the frosting off. I hardly even realize I'm doing it as I stare into those hypnotizing blue eyes. Yes, that's what wrong with me. I'm being hypnotized. It's not my fault, I can't control my actions. So when I wrap my lips around his digit and suck, it's not something I can stop. How can I when he's looking at me with such intensity?

Cooper slides his thumb out of my mouth and slowly trails it down the underside of my chin, my throat, and finally rests it on the hollow of my neck. I know he can feel the heat of my skin and my pulse racing. His eyes trace the same path back up to my lips, and then higher to meet my gaze. I can't quite place the look he's giving me. It's more than lust. More than longing. Could it be a different L-word?

Something about that breaks the spell. I step away from him, my heart hammering in my chest. What in the living hell is this man doing to me?

"I like that you always seem to have frosting on you," he grins as if he didn't just touch me in the most intimate way anyone has ever touched me. Pathetic? Maybe. True? Definitely.

I try coming up with some witty response, something both sexy and alluring, even though I know I shouldn't. But, instead of saying words, I snort. So, you know. There's that. I don't understand my behavior or why I want to impress him. Some part of me longs for him to want me, to touch me, to...

Cooper grins and leans against the counter with an easy, effortless posture. Ah, yes, this brings me back to reality. He makes everything look easy. It probably has been for his whole life.

Well, I won't be easy for him.

"What are you making, sweetness?"

I scowl at his pet name for me.

"I thought we already had this discussion. I'm not your sweetness. I'm not sweet. I'm all claws, remember?" I meant it to come out harshly, but instead, my voice is low and flirty. This man is breaking me. I don't like it.

Yes, you do.

No! Fuck.

"Ah, yes. My kitten. How could I forget? I think you're sweet too, though. You're just waiting for someone to break down those walls of yours."

I roll my eyes and turn back toward my cookies, ignoring his comment. I also ignore the way my heart lurches in my chest.

The hair on the back of my neck stands up. Cooper is behind me, so close I can smell his spicy, cinnamon scent. So close I can feel the warmth radiating off of his body. So close I can feel his breath on my skin.

I hold my breath as I wait for his next move. Cooper's lips ghost over the shell of my ear as his hands lightly hold my hips. My heart is beating so loudly I almost don't hear his words.

"I've already seen your tender heart you keep locked up tight. I don't know why you're so afraid, but I promise I'll never hurt you." Cooper kisses the side of my neck, making me close my eyes and dissolve into his touch. "I only want to protect you. Provide for you. Please you." His mouth moves down to the sensitive spot between my neck and shoulder, kissing me there as well. "You don't trust me yet, but I can be patient. I'll show you how good we can be together."

He ends his declaration by pressing his lips to my temple and breathing me in. I shouldn't let him touch me. I shouldn't *want* his touch the way I do. But I crave it. Cooper steps away from me and I feel cold and empty. I'm trembling slightly, the piping bag shaking in my hand.

I take a deep breath and center myself once again.

Don't get caught up in his game. You're finally starting life on your own, don't fuck it up by giving your heart away.

"Look, Cooper, I'm sure you're a good guy," I start. Might as well get this over with now before he touches me again and unravels me completely.

"Really? You don't seem so sure," he says, throwing me off guard.

"Actually, I can't get a read on you. But that's beside the point. I'm not a kept woman and I don't need your protection. Or your provision. In case you didn't notice, I have my own business and I'm doing just find providing for myself."

He looks like he wants to protest but changes his mind and smiles instead. "Speaking of your business, have you thought any more about my offer?"

"I already told you I don't want your help. With anything. Ever." I go back to decorating the cookies, feeling a calm wash over me. I can be annoyed with him. I feel like I have footing on solid ground once again, not drowning in the deep end like I was before.

"I hope to change that, kitten, I really do." I can't see his face, since I'm ultra-focused on these damn cookies, but I can hear the grin. I can even hear the dimple popping out.

"I'm not a kitten. I'm a fucking tiger, so you better step off," I growl.

Cooper chuckles, which makes me want to kick him in the knee. "You can be a tiger to everyone else, but to me, you are my kitten."

I spin around with my hands on my hips, dropping the piping bag and not giving a single shit about the wasted frosting. Right as I'm about to yell at him, Cooper backs up with his hands out in front of him.

"I'll leave before you can kick me out," he says, still smiling.

I scowl at him as he walks out of the back room. When I hear the bell ding, signaling he's left the shop, I take a deep breath and ignore the tightness in my chest.

Chapter 4

Cooper

I'm still buzzing from seeing Sienna yesterday. She was growly and feisty as fuck, but also vulnerable and fragile, though she has no idea I saw that side of her too. I took a risk the way I held her, peppered kisses on her delicate neck, and whispered my intentions in her ear. But I felt how she longed for my touch, the way her body softened in my hands. It told me everything I need to know. It's not just me in this thing. She feels it too. She just needs time. I can give her that.

While I wait for her to come to terms with the fact that she's mine, I'll hang on to these small moments. The little touches. The sparkle in her eyes when she lets me in just a little. The feel of her silky-smooth skin beneath my lips. Goddamn, when she licked my thumb and sucked on me? Fucking Christ, I swear I almost nutted in my damn pants. When I finally sink into her tight little pussy, I know it's going to be amazing. She's so damn tempting. So fucking sexy.

"Cooper!" Asher yells at me, startling me out of my thoughts. "What the hell is wrong with you lately? You're always a little..." he waves his hand around like he doesn't even have a word to describe me. "But these last few days it's like you're not even here."

Normally something like this would prompt me to give a snarky remark and piss my oldest brother off, but I don't want his shitty attitude to ruin my good mood. I look over at Declan, who is grinning and shaking his head at me. He knows what's up.

"Leave him alone, Ash," Declan says.

Asher looks at him like he grew a second head. Ash isn't used to people standing up to him or contradicting him. He's always been the de facto leader of the three of us, probably due to his sense of superiority being the eldest and all.

Despite all of us having equal shares and equal responsibility in the company, Asher has always called most of the shots. What he says goes around here. I'm fine letting him take charge if he wants to. I like my job, but I've always known life is about so much more than work. Declan used to be just as consumed by the job as Asher is, but then he met his Luna and got on my level with the correct priorities.

All that being said, typically our dynamic is that Asher is the iron fist and Declan supports his decisions while I make his life annoying in any way I can. That's not to say I don't take my job seriously or I don't care about the company. I can stand up and argue a point if I find it important enough. The few times I have, though, Declan and Asher team up and trample my ideas. Now, the power is shifting, so to speak. Declan is becoming less of a hardass, and more of a neutral figure. Still not a pushover by any means, but he's a little more balanced.

And Ash doesn't like it.

"I won't *leave him alone*. Not when his blasé attitude is threatening to ruin the company," Asher snaps.

"Psh, stop being so dramatic, brother," I say. "I'm not *ruining* the company. We're doing really well. After landing the Hashimoto account and killing it with the pitch to Fendi, we're way beyond reaching our goal of increasing profits by twenty percent. Plus, Declan and Luna getting married and starting a family has the board off of our backs. We have more inquiries than ever, we opened that new office in Chicago last month, and my team in research and development has been hard at work upping our targeted and in-line ads game."

Asher's normal scowl softens a bit as is eyebrows lift up slightly in surprise. Like I said, just because I'm more laid back doesn't mean I'm not good at what I do.

"Well..." Asher grunts. "Still doesn't mean we have any room to slack. The minute you're satisfied with where you are—"

"You aren't there anymore," both Declan and I finish for him.

"You gotta lay off dad's trite business quotes, Ash," I say.

"Trite? The man built this company from the ground up, you'd think that would earn him some respect."

"The man was a douche canoe, and you know it," I retort.

"Cooper..." Asher warns. He doesn't like anyone speaking ill of dad. He's loyal to a fault, though I suspect he caught the worst of dad's manipulation and harmful words. None of us survived our childhood without some warped views on life.

I put my hands up in a sign of surrender. Asher drones on about whatever the fuck he was saying before he yelled at me, while my mind wanders back to my little kitten.

More specifically, I think about ways I can promote her business. I know she said she didn't want my help, but I have to do something to prove that we are a good team and that I support her goals and dreams. What better way to do that than come alongside her and join forces to make her business more profitable? She clearly loves what she does, and I heard her when she said she didn't want to be a kept woman.

I almost pushed back when she told me that. Of course I don't want to keep her locked up and control her every move. Okay, I might want to keep her locked up, just a little bit, but I won't do that to her. I won't suffocate her or snuff out her spark. I knew my words would be empty, however, so I decided to let it go until I could think of some actions to back them up with.

And now I have it.

When the brain trust meeting is *finally* over, I go back to my office and email a client who runs an online magazine. I send her over a link to the Mad Batter Bakery Instagram page, along with a short write-up about what brief history I got out of Sienna the other day and the location of the bakery.

The reply came back a few hours later saying the article would be up tomorrow. Good. I'm that much closer to breaking through to Sienna.

***

The next day, I wait not so patiently, reloading the homepage of NYC Sweets every two minutes. Finally, *finally*, I see the article pop up.

There's a huge featured image of the cake Sienna made for Declan and Luna's wedding. I click into the article and see writer even called and got a quote from Luna about working with Sienna to create her dream cake. The article gives some background about how Sienna has been in New York for about a year and how she learned everything she knows from her grandma. The rest of the article is filled with images embedded from the bakery's Instagram, which really speaks for itself.

It's perfect. I'm sure Sienna will be getting calls for custom orders as soon as this afternoon. I want to go sit in her bakery all day and wait for her to figure it out. She'll probably be annoyed at first, but once she gets over her pride and business starts to pick up, she'll see I was right. Not that this is about that at all. I'm not about playing the *I told you so* game, especially not with her. I just want her to see I support her and am willing to do what it takes to see her succeed.

I stare at my phone, willing her to call me. I gave her my number all those days ago, but she has yet to use it. I hope she didn't throw the card away. It doesn't matter though. Soon enough we'll be married and spending all of our time together.

Declan emails me about a new client and I get caught up in the onboarding process. It's just as well. I need a distraction before I go fucking crazy. If I don't hear from Sienna by the end of the workday, I'll just drop by her shop.

Three hours later, my cell rings with an unknown number. It has to be her.

"Si—"

"What did you do?" she snaps.

I thought she'd be a little upset, but I'm shocked at the rage behind Sienna's voice.

"The artic—"

"I told you I didn't want your help!"

"Are you getting more business at least?" I have no idea where this anger is coming from, so I try to divert the attention away from me and back to her bakery.

"I don't want to be found," she says, a desperate edge to her tone. My heart stops in my fucking chest at her words. "The bakery, I mean," she's quick to say. "I don't want the bakery to...attract attention." I don't believe her for a second but I play along.

"Why wouldn't you want people to discover the bakery?"

"It's not all about money for everyone, you know. I like my business the way it is. I like being local, catering to people who care enough about small business to get to know me and my product."

What she's saying makes sense, on some level, and she has conviction behind her words. I didn't consider that she enjoyed her quiet bakery and that her lack of marketing was intentional. That being said, I think there's more to it than that. She wouldn't be so angry otherwise.

"Can I come over? I want to talk to you in person."

"No. Absolutely not."

"Please, kitten—"

"Don't call me that. I can't believe you did this. No, scratch that. I totally believe it."

Her words pierce me. Pain like I've never known spreads across my chest.

"Sienna, I swear my intentions were good. I'm so sorry I hurt you, please let me come over so we can talk."

"Your intentions mean fuck all right now, Cooper. I can't...shit, I can't..." Sienna sighs, the fight draining from her voice. "You have no idea what you've done." She sounds defeated and distant like she's playing out some scenario in her head.

"How can I fix this? Tell me what to do and it's done."

"Goodbye, Cooper."

"No, Sienna, please..." She already hung up. "FUCK!" I yell, gripping my phone tightly in my hand, resisting the urge to throw it against the wall. The only thing stopping me is the fact that she called me, which means I have her number now.

It takes everything in me not to call her right back. I know she wouldn't answer me anyway, and I don't want her to feel suffocated. Taking a calming breath, I try to think rationally about this and come up with a plan. Only, I can't think rationally when it comes to my Sienna. And game plans have never really been my thing.

Declan, on the other hand, is a planner. A few months ago, I would have scoffed at the idea of going to Declan for relationship advice, but Luna changed everything. I want to be the one to change everything for Sienna, but I realize now it has to be on her terms. I can't steamroll her. I can't *make* her trust me. She has to decide that on her own, and I didn't help my cause by going over her head and doing something she didn't want me to do.

There's more to her story, of that I am sure. But I can get to that later. Right now, I need to find Declan and get his help.

Chapter 5

Sienna

I closed the bakery after I got off the phone with Cooper. I'm livid and scared and trembling from the adrenaline coursing through my veins. Good thing Mandy's shift was already over by the time I figured out what Cooper did.

It started with a call for a custom order for some socialite's eighteenth birthday. Sure, I haven't done many custom orders in the time I've been open, but I expected some business after doing the cake for Luna and Declan. By the time the third custom order came in within the span of a few hours, I knew something was up. I asked the lady how she heard about Mad Batter, and she said there was an article online, NYC Sweets. My hand shook so hard I almost dropped the phone. I thanked her and grabbed my laptop.

Sure enough, there was an article posted a few hours earlier. Fear squeezed my heart and robbed me of my breath. There was enough information in the article for anyone to find me. I'm not so much worried about *anyone* finding me, though. I'm worried about *her* finding me. My mom. After our last conversation, seeing the state she was in, I have no doubts she'd figure out a way to get revenge by any means necessary.

I'm hunkered down in my apartment now, hiding under my covers like a coward. I can't help it. My body refuses to move even one inch. Every little noise makes me jump out of my skin. A thin sheen of sweat covers my body, but I don't remove my blankets. I know they won't actually protect me if anything happens, but it's something.

Stupid tears prick my eyes and I flinch when I hear someone pounding on the bakery door downstairs. I know it can't be her. Last time I checked, my mom's still in Cali, which means there's no way she could have gotten here this fast. But tell that to my anxiety.

"Sienna, please let me fix this."

It's Cooper. He sounds strained, frazzled, out of control. It's nothing like the easy-going, smug yet charming voice I'm used to from him. I ache all over just thinking about him, let alone being so close to him.

I didn't think he'd gotten so far under my skin, but each word of that article felt like a knife in my back. Even without all of the trying to stay hidden shit, the fact that he just ignored my requests and did whatever he wanted to do anyway only confirmed that he is the controlling, manipulative asshole I was worried about from the very beginning.

It shouldn't hurt this much, but god, it does. I wanted to believe him. I *did* believe him when he said he wouldn't hurt me, when he said he could be patient. Yeah, fucking right. If I weren't shackled to my bed by fear, I'd storm downstairs and claw his face off. I'd show him exactly how much of a *kitten* I am. How *sweet* I can be.

"Just tell me you're okay. I'm worried out of my goddamn mind. I've been texting you all night."

All night? I thought it was only three...

I look at my phone, ignoring the dozens of messages from Cooper, and see it's ten p.m. Shit. I didn't think I fell asleep, but hours are missing from my evening. More importantly, that means she could very well be here, looking for me. Waiting for me. She probably isn't. But it's not out of the realm of possibility.

"Baby, please. I don't want to, but I'll call the cops. I need to know you're okay. I fucked up. I know that. We don't have to talk; I just need to know you're okay."

I unlock my phone and scroll through Cooper's texts, not reading a single one. I type out a brief message.

Me: I'm fine.

Cooper: Thank you.

I wait for him to say something more, to grovel, I guess, or beg me or promise me the world, but he doesn't. Which is fine. I just want him to go away. Don't I? Why am I listening for his voice downstairs? Why do I suddenly feel so lonely knowing he's walking away?

***

I didn't open the bakery the next day. Or the day after. I told Mandy I was sick and she could have the rest of the week off.

This morning, however, I woke up with a newfound determination. Mother hasn't come knocking at my door yet, which means she probably didn't see the article and I've been freaking out for no reason. Even if she is after me, I refuse to live in fear anymore. Too much of my life was wasted hiding away.

I woke up this morning and stared down at the first tattoo I got, the day I turned eighteen. It's on the inside of my forearm, right below the crook of my elbow.

Be you, bravely.

From that day forward, I did what I had to do to get the fuck out of the life I was living. Worked two jobs, stole money from my mom's loser boyfriends, even sold some pills my mom scored from the dealer she was fucking at the time. I'm not proud of that last one, but I was desperate.

No matter what I did, how much I made, how much I saved, I still couldn't get out of the trailer park we lived in. Oakland felt more and more like a prison with each passing day. My mom was getting worse, so I ended up paying the bills. Turns out she took a few credit cards out in my name and proceeded to max them out. I was saddled with debt from the moment I was legally an adult.

All of that changed when my Grams died. Even though she only lived across the water in San Francisco, I didn't get to see her much. Our visits went from once every few weeks, to every few months, and then just on holidays. I know mom had a lot to do with that, and I don't blame Grams for not wanting to fight with her all the time. It hurt, nonetheless, to feel abandon by the only person in my life who liked me. When she died right after my nineteenth birthday, she left everything to me. Her house, her life insurance money, her savings, family heirlooms. All of it was mine.

And I knew just what to do with it. I moved as far away as I could and started a bakery. *My bakery*. I won't let anyone or anything take it away from me.

I finally roll out of bed and take a few deep breaths before getting dressed and heading downstairs to the shop.

I yelp in surprise when I see a large figure standing by the front door, but then sigh with relief when I see it's Cooper. My heart still beats out of control, but it's not so much out of fear.

I unlock the door and open it up to find the man I can't help but miss. Cooper. He's as stunning as ever, of course, but he looks a bit run down.

"Sienna," he says, sounding relieved.

"Cooper," I respond, trying to sound neutral. "What are you doing here?"

"I've been here the last two mornings, hoping to catch you. But you haven't been around."

I nod but don't offer any other information. There's a sticky note on the front door from UPS, saying I missed a package yesterday, but they'd be back this afternoon to deliver it. Strange. I don't remember ordering anything.

"How are you doing? I mean, are you...is everything okay?"

I look over my shoulder at Cooper, who is rubbing the back of his head in a nervous gesture. I want to be mad at him. And I am. But I can't deny the fact that I feel safer now that he's around. I'd like to shoo him off, but I want to soak up a little more of his comfort while I still can.

"I'm fine. Just needed a few days to myself."

"Can we talk? I feel like you're not telling me something. Are you in danger?"

"No," I lie. "I just hate that you went behind my back. I hate that you ignored my wishes and did whatever the fuck you wanted to do. I know men like you, men who push an agenda, men who can't take no for an answer." Well, so much for not pushing him away. I'm sure he's going to walk out now, taking all of his warmth with him.

Cooper doesn't say anything, so I turn around to look at him. I'm shocked to see he looks absolutely stricken. I have the urge to hug him, but I don't.

"Fuck," he whispers. "I did that." His brow is furrowed in anguish, and he's more talking to himself than to me.

"Cooper..." I don't know what to say, but my stupid heart is breaking at seeing him like this.

He looks up at me, and I swear I see unshed tears in his eyes. It almost makes me want to cry, seeing him in this much pain.

"Baby, I'm so sorry. I know you have no reason to believe me, but I swear to you, I'm not that guy. I wanted to show you that we would make a good team, that I want to support your goals and you won't ever be a kept woman. But I understand I violated your trust."

I shouldn't believe him, but God help me, I do. It doesn't change the fact that he could have potentially put me in harm's way, but I believe him when he says he just wanted good things for me and my business.

I'm overcome with so many emotions, but I can't seem to voice any of them. I give Cooper a curt nod and continue walking to the back room so I can start baking.

Since I've been out for the last two days, I have a lot to do if I want to open on time. That makes me realize what time it is, and specifically, that Cooper was already outside of the door when I got downstairs.

"You've been here the last two mornings." It's a statement, not a question.

"Yeah. I wanted to see you face to face."

"But it's barely four-thirty in the morning."

Cooper shrugs, following me into the back room. He starts getting pans out for me and measuring cups. I don't need half the stuff he's pulling out of drawers and shelves, but it's a sweet gesture all the same.

"It's not like I was sleeping anyway," he says, grabbing the five-pound bag of flour I was reaching for.

"Why not?"

He stares at me for a second, like he's trying to figure me out.

"Because I fucked things up with you," he says as if it's obvious. "Because every hour I didn't see you or hear from you felt like my heart was being ripped out of my chest. I actually thought I was having a heart attack last night, but it turns out it was a panic attack. I couldn't stand the thought of never seeing you again. I'm so fucking sorry, Sienna."

I don't even know what to say to all of that. He really does care about me, that much is evident. He looks like he hasn't slept in days. I can hear the exhaustion and pain in his voice. I look in his deep blue eyes, seeing the way they're pleading for me to give him another chance. The man had a fucking panic attack, the least I can do is let him hang around and talk if that's what he wants, right? I hear the voice in the back of my head telling me not to fall for it, not to let anyone inside, not to give him even one inch of space in my heart.

The thing is, fuck that voice. Time to be me, bravely.

I reach out for his hand, squeezing it softly. His eyes dart down to our connected hands, shock covering his features.

"It's okay, Cooper. I forgive you."

He heaves out a huge breath like he's been holding it since I first called him three days ago.

Cooper lifts my hand to his lips and presses the softest kiss over my knuckles.

"Thank you, sweetness," he whispers into the skin of my hand.

I try to fight my smile at his endearment, but I lose the battle. At least I succeed in rolling my eyes at him.

"So, what can I do to help?" He asks, letting go of my hand. I shove away the feeling of loss when we break contact.

"Don't you have work in a few hours? You should go home and sleep or something before you go to the office."

"Nah, I took a few days off. I'm the least important brother, so it's fine." He winks at me, but I can tell he's not entirely joking. It's weird seeing him insecure about something. I don't like it.

"I'm sure that's not true. You have the ability to boost businesses by sending one article into circulation. I'm sure that kind of pull gets you pretty far in marketing, huh?" I meant it as a joke, but Cooper looks like I stabbed him in the gut. "Hey, I was kidding. Too soon?"

He quickly recovers, shaking his head and smiling. Yes, this is the Cooper I know. I don't like it when he's not smiling. I want him to always be happy around me. I try not to dwell on that thought for too long, however.

"If you're serious about helping, you can clean up the front. Wipe down tables, sweep, clean out the bakery case. Then come back to me for your next assignment," I wink at him.

He grins and snakes an arm around my waist. I gasp as he hauls me into his chest and tucks some hair that came out of my messy bun behind my ear.

"You're bossy," he says, smiling down at me.

"You like it," I grin up at him. I can't help it. That smile of his is contagious.

"Love that smile, sweetness," he murmurs before kissing my forehead.

It's such a tender moment. Tears threaten to spill out of my eyes, so I shove off of him, swatting his chiseled chest and telling him to get to work.

The two of us actually do make a pretty good team, and I won't lie, I like bossing him around. It gives me immense joy to order around a six-foot-three wall of sexy man. I love when he looks over at me, waiting for his next instruction. Cooper isn't the arrogant man I thought he was.

We get into a good rhythm, even after the shop opens. Cooper hops on the register and picks everything up in no time. The morning rush comes and goes, and Cooper heads out to the lobby to clean up again.

The bell rings at the door, and I turn to see a delivery man walking through. I step out to sign for the package and offer the delivery guy a cookie on the house. I catch Cooper smiling at me and fight the blush threatening to creep into my cheeks.

I take the package back to the counter and grab a box cutter. The return address isn't one I recognize, but the package has my name right on the front.

Not the bakery name. *My* name.

My stomach drops even before I open the package.

With shaky hands, I lift the flaps of the box and dig through the packing peanuts to find a soft, stuffed bunny. I sink to the floor, unable to breathe.

She found me. She knows where I live, where I work. She's tormenting me, something she was always very skilled at.

"Sienna? Baby, what's wrong?" Cooper sounds like he's shouting at me underwater.

I can't hear anything other than a high-pitched ringing in my ear and my frantic heartbeat. Everything goes blurry. I'm vaguely aware of a warmth pressing against me. Then I hear another heartbeat, steady, calming, grounding.

I come back into my body and realize Cooper is holding me in his lap and stroking my back. My face is pressed against his chest, my hand over his heart.

"You're okay, I've got you, Sienna, I'm right here," he whispers over and over.

I'm shaking all over, tears streaming down my face as I snot all over Cooper's shirt. God, I'm a mess. "Sorry," I squeak out.

"What's going on, sweetness?" He asks, peeling me off his chest.

I panic and grab his shirt, pulling myself back into his warmth. I bury my face in the side of his neck because apparently, I can't function without being in his arms.

"It's alright, sweetness. I've got you," he says, his hand moving up my back to massage my neck in calming circles.

Before I can process what's happening, Cooper stands up with me in his arms. I cling to him as he pulls me closer. I should tell him I'm fine, that he needs to leave so I can pack up my life and get the hell out of Dodge. But the thought of leaving Cooper has a fresh wave of tears coating my lashes.

He carries me upstairs, where I forgot to lock the door to my apartment, and walks inside, setting me down on the couch. "I'm gonna go close up, okay? I'll be back in a few minutes," he says in a warm, calming voice.

I nod and curl up on the couch. Cooper looks so worried. Normally that would piss me off, but right now I just want someone to be with me. Not just anyone though; I want Cooper. He looks torn between hugging me again and going downstairs. Eventually, he kisses me on the temple and runs downstairs to lock up.

By the time he returns, I've gotten myself together a bit. I'm embarrassed that he saw me lose my shit. I have to put up a strong front and get him to go away. I can't afford to get any closer to him if I'm just going to leave.

Cooper sits down next to me, but I refuse to look at him. He makes me feel so many vulnerable things, and right now, I need to be tough.

"Sienna," he starts. "You want to tell me about this?"

I don't mean to, but I look over at him. More specifically, I look over at the faded purple bunny he's holding in his hand. It's missing an eye and all of the stuffing in its left leg came out years ago. I grab the bunny and run my fingers over the threadbare fabric of its belly, and then up to circle its cold, shiny nose.

Seeing the stuffed toy up close breaks something open deep inside of me. This bunny has soaked up so many of my tears. We moved from trailer to trailer together, endured drunken fights between mom and her boyfriends. We've suffered more than our fair share of bruises. It all comes bubbling up to the surface in this moment, the unfairness of it all, the secrets, the shame, the bitterness, the fear.

"This is Tulip," I whisper. "I got her when I was four."

Chapter 6

Cooper

Sienna is lost in a memory as she toys with the purple bunny's ears. She looks so fucking fragile right now, though I can tell she's trying to be brave and detached. I have to know what the hell is going on, but I don't want to push too hard and have her shut me out completely.

I wasn't lying when I told her I've hardly slept the last few days. It took everything in me not to beat down her door and demand her to accept my apology. I figured that wouldn't win me any points towards convincing her I'm not a steamrolling control freak.

I don't know what I would have done if I didn't see Sienna this morning. Yeah, I'm exhausted, and I ache without her, but more than that, I was going out of my goddamn mind with worry. Thank fuck she saw something in my eyes when I apologized this morning. The way she looked at me like no one had ever worried about her or cared about her just about broke my heart. I want to know every single thing about her, why she has these walls, why she thinks she needs to push good things away. But I'll settle for why an old stuffed bunny sent her into a tailspin.

The late morning sun streams through the window and lights up Sienna's features in a warm glow. Her delicate brow furrows as she studies the stuffed toy in her hand. I want to ask her a million questions, but I don't want to scare her off. Instead, I sit back and wait for her to gather her thoughts. I can only do so much to make her trust me. At some point, she has to be the one to take the leap.

"This is Tulip," she whispers. "I've had her since I was four."

I lean closer but resist the urge to touch her. She needs space and I'll try to give that to her. Hopefully, my presence is enough.

"My mom…" she trails off and closes her eyes. I notice her fingers digging into the bunny as she grips it tightly. "I was an unwelcome surprise when my mom was barely eighteen, and she never missed an opportunity to remind me of that. I was always too clingy, or too awkward, or too annoying. I was too much, always too much."

Her voice is quiet and unsure. I've never seen her so vulnerable. This is Sienna with all of her walls down. This is her showing me all of her painful parts. I swear to fucking Christ I will cover her with my strength and protect her always. I'll make sure she knows she's not too much, that she's perfect, and worthy, and *mine*.

"She resented that she had to spend money on me instead of drugs, though there were plenty of those around too," Sienna continues, laughing bitterly. "And it's not like she didn't have her pick of men who wanted to load her up and use her body."

There's so much to unpack in those two sentences. I want to ask about the loser boyfriends, what the money situation was like, if she got enough to eat, if her friends or teachers knew about her home life, and if so, how the hell they could have let her stay there. I try not to say anything, but one question slips out of my mouth.

"Drugs?" I choke out.

Sienna nods. "Mostly fentanyl and oxy, though she dated a meth head once and tried that for a hot second. Yikes," she shudders. "Anyway. My mom might have hated me, but my Grams and I got along. As you know, she taught me to bake. She was so patient with me, teaching me both the chemistry and the art behind baking. I used to spend weekends with her in San Francisco until my mom stole a bunch of jewelry from her. Our visits became less and less, and eventually, she just sort of...I don't know. We lost touch."

Her shoulders sag. I can see it still hurts her to think about it. Jesus, the one person she counted on, probably the only person who really knew what went on behind the closed doors of her home, abandoned her over some stupid family drama. No wonder she doesn't want to depend on anyone ever again.

Sienna is quiet for a few moments, her grip easing up on the stuffed toy ever so much. It seems once she actually started talking, it got easier for her to find the words.

"My high school graduation present was a mountain of debt from cards my mom took out in my name. I worked as many jobs as I could to save up and get the fuck out of that shitty trailer, but it was one setback after another. When I turned nineteen, mom said I should have been paying rent since the moment I turned eighteen, so I owed her a year's worth of back rent. I snuck out that night with what little money I had in tow, but she caught me. Or, well, her boyfriend, Derek, caught me. Broke my arm so I couldn't waitress for a few weeks. I lost that job and got stuck renting my room in the trailer."

"Jesus," I grunt, trying to swallow down the string of curse words and death threats just on the tip of my tongue.

Every muscle in my body tenses as my veins fill with more rage than I knew I was capable of feeling. I'm the chill brother, the easy-going brother, the one who cracks a joke and breaks the tension. But hearing Sienna talk about her childhood, her manipulative mother, and now some fucker laying hands on her? All my calmness is gone. I want to make him pay for what he did. I don't just want to physically fuck him up, I want to *ruin* him and anyone else who caused Sienna harm.

Taking a deep breath, I scrub my hands down my face and try to focus on my kitten. I still don't know the connection between what she's told me and that bunny she's currently petting absent-mindedly in her lap. Right now, she looks like a little kid again. Scared and lost and clinging on to some semblance of safety and familiarity.

"A few months later, I got a letter requesting my presence at the reading of Deborah Carmichael's will."

I raise an eyebrow at her.

"My Grams," she whispers. Sienna turns her head and I pretend not to see her wiping a tear from her eye. Soon my girl won't be shy about showing me all of her emotions, but for now, I can give her some privacy.

She clears her throat and continues on. "Turns out Grams left me everything. Her house, her savings, all of it. There was a letter for me, too, she..." Sienna stops short like she suddenly revealed too much. "Anyway. The point is that Grams left it all to me. It was enough money to move across the country and start a new life. I knew right away I'd open a bakery and I always wanted to live in New York. I spent the next few months dealing with my grandma's estate, working with the lawyer, researching and trying to make well-informed choices when I sold the house and her things. I thought I was being careful with my outings and my phone calls, but mom's boyfriend found out."

"This the same dead man who broke your arm?" I growl.

Sienna raises her eyebrows in shock like she can't believe someone is upset on her behalf.

"Uh, yeah. Derek. At first, they were really sweet. Too sweet. I didn't know they knew about the money at the time, but Derek and my mom were being so nice to me and I guess...I don't know, I guess some stupid part of me wanted to believe maybe my mom loved me after all and that we could be a family. Pathetic, right? I was even considering moving them out here with me."

God, I want to touch her so bad right now. I want to hold her and shield her and love her in all of the ways she's never been loved before. I hate her mom, though I will always be grateful she gave Sienna life.

"You're not stupid or pathetic. Everyone needs love, sweetness. Especially those of us who went without it for so long."

"But I had nineteen years of experience showing me that I'm unlovable. How did I not put two and two together? They just so happen to start being nice to me once I became worth three hundred thousand dollars? I mean, fuck," she sighs, exasperatedly. "Wait. You said *us*?"

"Huh?"

"You said, 'those of *us* that went without love for so long.'"

"I did, didn't I. I want to tell you everything about me, and I will, in time. Right now I need to know why this bunny made my kitten cry."

Her lip ticks up just a little bit in one corner, helping to ease the tension a bit.

"It's not so much the bunny, but what it represents."

"Oh, great, that answers all of my questions," I joke.

She glares at me and hits me in the chest with the stuffed toy, grinning the whole time. I grab the bunny and pull Sienna into me, wrapping her up in my arms and kissing the top of her head. God, it feels good having her here. The best part is, she doesn't fight me. Not one bit. In fact, she sighs and snuggles closer.

"I heard my mom and Derek talking one morning when they thought I was still asleep. Mom said she was going to take me out for a girls' night and get me drunk and ask for a bunch of money. I was so furious with myself for falling for their shit."

She's shaking in my arms, and what she doesn't say is that she was more than pissed, more than furious. She was cut deep and it hurt more than she wants to admit, maybe even more that she's able to realize right now.

"I decided enough was enough. I booked a flight for New York then and there. When I refused to go out with my mom and instead started packing, she sort of...she sort of went ape shit on me."

"What did she do, sweetness?"

"It doesn't matter. She just made it clear she'd get the money from me one way or another."

I squeeze her tightly and drop another kiss on top of her head. "It matters, baby. You matter. Tell me what happened."

I need to know the extent of what I'm dealing with here so I know how best to protect her and her business. I also need to know the damage that was done to Sienna. Whatever her mother did and said caused some scars, whether she's willing to acknowledge them or not.

"She...Cooper, I've never seen her like that. I don't even know how to describe it. She was unhinged. Rabid. Literally clawing at me and ripping my clothes off. At some point, Derek grabbed a knife. There was so much yelling. *Sienna, you selfish cunt, you owe me for your life. Ungrateful bitch. Stupid whore. Worthless piece of garbage...*"

Sienna sniffles into my chest as my heart is torn in fucking two for my girl. I'm more determined than ever to shatter those lies and build her back up. I'll tell her every day how strong and precious she is to me.

"My mom told me if I wouldn't give her the money, she'd kill me and it would all default to her since she's my only living relative. I don't know if I believe she'd actually do that, or if she can even get it together enough to form any sort of plan, but Derek is no fool. He's more capable than people give him credit for. I relented and told them I needed a few days to finish up liquidating the assets. In a show of good faith, I gave my mom five thousand dollars that night, knowing she'd use it to get super fucked up. When she and Derek passed out, I left for the airport and never looked back. I've been trying to keep a low profile this last year. I should have just disappeared and taken some waitressing job or something, but I wanted to do something with my life that I could be proud of, you know?"

It finally dawns on me why she was so livid about the article.

"And I fucked it all up with that article, didn't I?"

Sienna stiffens in my arms and pulls away from me. I feel the loss of her immediately, but I give her this space if she needs it. She wipes off her face, still trying to hide from me behind a curtain of her hair.

"It had my name and location, and, well, it's no coincidence that my childhood stuffed toy ended up being sent to me a few days later."

"Sienna..." I choke back the swell of regret threatening to make me cry or puke or punch a damn wall. I hate myself so much in this moment. "I'm so sorry. I didn't know. But that's no excuse. I didn't listen when you said you didn't want me to market your business, and

I should have respected that regardless of your reasons. Fuck, baby, I'm so sorry."

She tucks her knees up to her chest and wraps her arms around them, making herself as small as possible. I can just picture her doing that in her childhood room, trying to disappear while her mom got high. I hate that I'm the one who did that to her.

"It's okay, Cooper. I forgave you. I don't say shit I don't mean."

Despite the guilt and anger and hurt rushing through my body, I smile at her words. She's too fucking perfect and she's letting me in. Finally.

"It's not okay, kitten, but I'm going to fix it, I promise."

"You don't have to do anything, Cooper. It's not your mess."

"It *is* my mess. I literally delivered you right into a harmful situation. But even if it wasn't my fault, it'd still be my mess because it's *you* who's in trouble. Your problems are my problems. Your struggles are my struggles. Just like your victories are my victories. I want to support you in every way, and right now that means protecting you. I know you don't trust easily, but I'm asking you to trust me. Let me take care of you, Sienna. Let me in, baby, let me protect you."

"Cooper, I..."

"Let me show you how much you mean to me, how serious I am about us."

I can practically see her thoughts as she battles them out in her mind. There's nothing more I can say right now. She has to give herself to me, to my protection.

Only a few moments have passed, but it feels like an eternity while she fights her demons behind closed eyes. Sienna shocks the hell out of me by launching into my arms. I catch her and hold her close while she straddles me and buries her face in my neck.

"Don't hurt me," she pleads, her voice soft and broken.

"Never, sweetness. Never again," I vow.

Sienna places a sweet kiss on the side of my neck that has me feeling all sorts of things. I cup the back of her neck and draw her head up so I can look into her beautiful hazel eyes and make her believe me.

God, I want to say so many things but she's not ready to hear any of them. *I love you, you're mine, we're never going to be apart from this moment forward.*

Looking at her now, though, I know she understands. Just like I can see to the very depths of her being and know she is handing me all of her brokenness, her heartache, her pain. She's also giving me her hopes, her happiness, her future.

I cup her face with one hand and stroke her cheek with my thumb. She leans into my touch and parts her sweet lips. I take a minute to savor this connection, to feel the weight of what's happening between us. Once I taste her, there will be no going back for me, not ever.

She closes the distance between us, kissing me first. It's every-fucking-thing that she wants this too. I sip at her soft lips, taking first her top lip into my mouth, and then her bottom lip, switching back and forth until she opens up for me and allows me to slip my tongue inside of her sweet, inviting mouth. I explore her depths in long, languid strokes, loving the way she relaxes into me.

I angle her head and deepen our kiss, unable to get enough of her. My fingers tangle in her hair and pull her closer to me. My other hand slides up her thigh, her hip, and rests on her lower back, keeping her soft curves pressed against me.

Sienna starts rocking against my hardening cock, making me groan into her sexy little mouth. Her hands explore my body, squeezing my shoulders, my biceps, and drifting down to the hem of my shirt. The sweetest of sighs escapes her lips and her hands slip under my shirt to rest against my torso. I feel each finger uncurl and clench into my skin. Her nails bite into my flesh almost to the point of pain, which only fuels my desire for her.

I break our kiss and drag air into my lungs while still nipping and kissing down her jaw and neck. Sienna tilts her head to the side to give me better access. I groan in approval and continue to devour her sensitive skin, loving the taste of her on my tongue. She's all sugar and spice, just like I thought.

Making my way back up her neck and jaw, I take her lips again in a punishing kiss, claiming her and showing her who she belongs to whether she's ready to admit it or not. When we break apart, I rest my forehead on hers, my hand still at the back of her neck keeping her close to me.

Fuck, this woman is ruining me in the best way possible.

"Do you trust me?" I whisper.

She nods against my forehead.

"Need your words, kitten."

"I trust you, Cooper."

I breathe a sigh of relief and press a soft kiss on her lips.

"I want you to stay with me. It's not safe for you here. You can have your own room and bathroom. There's plenty of space for the two of us. I don't want you here, sweetness. That means the bakery, too. I can't stand the thought of you being here all alone when there's a threat to your safety."

I expect her to push back or make excuses for why she can't. Instead, Sienna's eyes well up with tears and she nods in agreement. "Okay," she breathes out. "I don't want to be alone anymore."

"Never again, baby girl. I'm here now," I promise.

We stay like that for a long time, me holding her close while she rests her head on my shoulder. Eventually, we get up and I help her pack a few things before heading out to my car. She doesn't say anything as we pass through the bakery, but I can feel her thinking and worrying about what's going to become of the business she's built. I don't have the answers yet, but I'll come up with something. She'll have everything she's ever wanted and more.

***

Sienna crashed as soon as I showed her to the guest bedroom. I want her in my bed, *our* bed, but it's too soon, I know. I left her to get settled in and she was all curled up in a ball, fast asleep when I went and checked on her. I wanted nothing more than to curl up around her and shield her from the world, but I had work to do.

I called Declan, and yes, even Asher to discuss some options on what to do with the bakery. Shutting down would ruin her business, especially after she's been getting more custom orders. Part of me wants to lock her away and tell her I'll build her a new bakery anywhere she wants with a top of the line kitchen and anything else she can dream up as soon as all of this shit with her mom blows over. But I know that's not the solution.

It took some convincing, but Ash finally agreed to my plan and Declan drew up the documents and emailed them to me. It's been a few hours, and hopefully Sienna will be up sooner rather than later. I decide to make dinner for us in the meantime.

As if summoned by the smell of steak and potatoes, Sienna appears in the doorway of the kitchen, looking all adorable and sleepy in her yoga pants and a baggy sweatshirt. Her hands play at the hem of her shirt and she chews on her bottom lip in a nervous gesture.

I'm sitting at the table after just plating our food in hopes she'd join me soon.

"Come here, sweetness," I say, giving her a warm smile to ease her discomfort.

She pads her cute little feet over to me and starts to sit down on the seat next to me. I reach out and grab her hips, directing her to sit on my lap instead. Sienna plops down and looks at me over her shoulder, one eyebrow raised.

I kiss the tender spot below her ear, making her sigh.

"Let's eat. Then we can talk about the next steps, okay?"

"I am perfectly capable of eating on my own, you know," she says with a little bit of attitude.

I just wrap my arms around her waist and nip her earlobe. "I know, baby. But you're in my care now, remember?"

I can't see her face since she's turned away from me, but I swear I can hear her rolling her eyes. I think she likes me taking charge, taking care of her, but she can't quite admit it yet. After all, she has yet to make a move to get out of my lap. I reach around her and cut up a piece of steak.

"You're bossy," she says, though there's no venom in her words.

"You'll get used to it," I tease, lifting the steak up to her luscious lips. She sighs in exasperation but accepts the food.

Sienna lets me feed her the entire plate of food, and only then do I grab the other plate and eat dinner myself while she leans back on my chest. When I'm done, I scoop her up in my arms, making her squeal in surprise. I sit on the couch with her still in my arms. I can't explain it, I just need to have her with me, on me, touching me all the fucking time. She doesn't seem to mind.

"So, what do we do now?" She asks after a few minutes of me just holding her and feeling her heartbeat against mine.

"Hear me out, okay? We can discuss the details, but I want to get all of this out there before you freak out."

"You know that's like... The worst way to start off a conversation, right?" Sienna grins, making me grin as well.

"My bad. What I meant to say was, I have an exciting business opportunity for you if I could get just a few minutes of your time."

"Mmhm..." she eyes me skeptically, but there's a hint of a grin still on her lips.

"I talked to my brothers and we want to temporarily purchase Mad Batter Bakery from you." She opens her mouth to protest, but I cut her off. "Hear me out, remember?" Sienna pouts and I can't help but kiss her cute little lips. "I have the paperwork printed off, right here with me. You can look it over. The contract explicitly states that you maintain complete creative control, every decision is still yours, and you can buy it back from us at any time for half of what we initially offer, which by the way, is two hundred thousand."

"So, wait. You're essentially buying my bakery in name only, and I can still run everything the way I want?" I nod. "And then I can buy it back and still keep one hundred thousand dollars?"

"Exactly."

"Why?"

"Two reasons. First of all, we can safely assume from the events that unfolded today, your mom and Derek are after you. Selling the business and moving in with me gives the appearance of you going on the run. It may deter them just enough if they show up and see the place is under new ownership. You know, get them off your trail and all that until I can deal with them more permanently."

Sienna looks like she's going to protest again, but I cut her off with another chaste kiss before continuing. "And second of all, I heard you when you said you don't want to be a kept woman. This is the only thing I could think of that would keep you safe and keep your business going without you taking a hit. You can bake everything here and we'll deliver stuff in the mornings. You can do your custom orders here and everything. God knows I paid enough for this huge kitchen that I don't use nearly often enough. Plus, when all is said and done, you'll have a nest egg that's all yours and no one, not me, not my brothers, not your mom, absolutely no one can touch except for you. And you'll have your bakery."

Sienna takes it all in, the wheels clearly turning in her head. It's a big ask of her, I know. Not only is she trusting me with her safety, but her livelihood as well. Plus, she'll be accepting a large sum of money at the end, which I know goes against every bone in her body.

She looks down at her lap, her hands twisting and untwisting as she gets lost in thought. I cover her small hands with mine, causing her to look up at me.

"When all is said and done?" She asks in a whisper.

"Yeah. My brothers and I have a certain pull within powerful circles, and I have no doubts we will be able to track down your mom and her low-life boyfriend. Once the threat is over, you'll have your business back and you'll have the money."

"Will I have you?"

God, her tentative voice and doubts break me apart. At the same time though, it gives me overwhelming hope that she wants to keep me at the end of all of this. I'm not just a white knight, so to speak, riding in to save the day.

"Of course, kitten. I'm yours. I told you I'm not going anywhere, and I meant it."

She nuzzles into the side of my neck and sighs.

"Okay," she breathes out.

"Thank fuck," I say, resting my head on hers. "Thank you for trusting me. I promise we'll get through this, okay?"

Sienna nods and I wrap her up in my arms. I can't believe the difference between the hostile woman who lashed out at me this morning and the vulnerable woman resting peacefully in my arms right now. I have no idea what I did to deserve her in my life, but one thing is for certain. I'm never letting her go now that she's here.

Chapter 7

Sienna

I spent the night in Cooper's guest room last night, though a part of me wanted nothing more than to crawl into his king-sized bed and have him hold me all night long. I spent so much time in his arms yesterday, but it didn't bother me. In fact, it only made me want more of it. More of him. It's been so long since anyone treated me with such kindness, probably since my Grams. And even then, Cooper's touch is more than just caring and gentle. It's reverent and calming and everything I've been missing in my life.

And don't even get me started on that kiss yesterday. It was sweet and full of emotion, but also hot and dirty and made my pussy ache to be filled for the first time. I have no doubts that Cooper will be my first everything. But I felt totally wrung out after the impossible day I had yesterday. I was in no state of mind or body to be giving myself over to lust, even in Cooper's capable hands.

We're headed to the notary right now in Cooper's ridiculous sports car. I already gave him a hard time about it, but he took everything in stride. We park and head up to the office, hand in hand.

Cooper signs and initials, and then hands me the pen. I don't realize my nerves until I'm putting the pen to paper with a shaky hand. He reaches out and covers it with both of his.

"Look at me, kitten," he whispers. I'm sure the lady watching us sign can hear him, but fuck if I care. I need to hear whatever words of affirmation I just know he's going to say. "I promise to always take care of you. This is only temporary, remember? You have all the power here, I'm just doing what I can to support you."

I nod and take a deep breath, even managing to give him a small smile. I sign and initial and then the lady signs as our witness, making the contract official.

"Let's go to lunch, sweetness. Declan and Luna invited us to one of their favorite places," Cooper says once we get back to the car.

"They know about us?"

Cooper looks at me with a sheepish smile. It's kind of adorable.

"Yeah...I may have told them I met the woman of my dreams right after you slapped me and left."

"Oh yeah?" I can't help but smirk at him, one eyebrow raised. "You may have?"

He grabs me and pulls me in for a passionate kiss. "I definitely told them that. There's no hiding how I feel about you, kitten," he says once we break for air.

"Well, in that case, I guess we shouldn't keep them waiting," I smile up at him.

He lingers for a moment more, his arms circled around my waist, looking me up and down. It sets my body on fire, enough to melt my heart. And my panties. I'm tired of fighting it. I want this man like nothing else. I want to give him everything – my body, my heart, my fucking soul. It should be terrifying, especially after a lifetime of keeping those parts of me protected, but Cooper just... He just snuck right in and set up camp in the very depths of my soul. I felt it the very first day I met him.

As if sensing the seismic shift in my heart, Cooper looks over and gives me one of his soft smiles. He gathers my hand up in his, lacing our fingers together and setting them on his lap while he drives to lunch.

When we arrive, I immediately feel out of my depth. And not in a good way. For starters, there's a valet. We are greeted at the door by a beautiful, leggy blonde who takes one look at me and turns her nose up in the air. Fair enough. I'm in jeans and a plain v-neck t-shirt. Cooper is dressed similarly in dark, form-fitting jeans and a Henley complete with a leather jacket, but his clothes look like he spent a couple thousand dollars on them, whereas mine look like... well, they look like I got them at Goodwill a few years ago. Which I did. The jeans have holes in them, but not the purposeful kind. And my shoes...still the ratty Vans.

The rational part of my brain knows that no one is probably looking at me. But the other part of my brain, the one currently in control, is acutely aware of the wingtip shoes, the Hermès bags, the designer dresses, and the five hundred dollar haircuts surrounding me. I can't remember the last time I got my hair cut. Certainly not since I've been in New York, that's for sure.

I like to think that I don't scare easily, that I've endured enough by now to not give a fuck what others think about me. Turns out I'm a lot weaker than I think.

Cooper drapes a protective arm over me as we head to the table. My initial reaction is to shove him away and run for the hills, but this is Cooper, and I find I kind of like him watching over me. Caring for me. Bossing me around. Dammit.

We get to the table where Declan and Luna are already seated. I don't have another second to feel awkward, because Luna stands up and throws her arms around me, pulling me in for a hug. I'm too shocked to respond at first, but then I soften a bit and hug her back. I have no idea how to receive this kind of friendship and familiarity.

Luna, however, doesn't seem to notice. She's as bright and bubbly as ever, wearing a light green blouse paired with pastel pink dress slacks. The outfit is topped off with a glittery white belt. She's freaking adorable and I look like a street urchin. I don't even have makeup on. In fact, I didn't pack any when I left my apartment to stay with Cooper.

With a reassuring hand at the small of my back, Cooper guides me to my chair before sitting down next to me. He keeps a hand on my thigh, squeezing lightly like he knows I'm feeling a little anxious.

"So," Luna says, her eyes practically glittering with giddiness as she fixes her gaze on me from across the table. "Sienna, I didn't get a chance to thank you for the cake. You ran away before I even noticed you were at the reception! You should have stayed for dinner."

"She ran into Coop, so I can understand why she felt the need to head for the nearest exit," Declan says.

"Hey, now. That was the best moment of my life," he replies easily. He looks over at me and grins. "The running into you part. Not the part where you ran away," he clarifies.

I roll my eyes but can't help the heat that spreads to my face. "I liked the part where I slapped you," I shoot back.

Luna coughs on her water, and Declan is right there to pat her on the back.

"She slapped you?" Declan smirks at Cooper before turning his gaze on me. "I think you'll be good for him."

I don't know what to say to that, so I sip my water, hoping no one sees my hand shake. Cooper must take the hint, the man knows how to read me inside and out, after all, and he changes the subject. We order our food and talk about Luna and Declan's baby who is due in about eight months. Luna tells us about her college classes and her brother, Lucas.

Cooper pipes in every now and then and Declan just looks at Luna like she's the most beautiful, precious thing in the whole world. I know that look. It's similar to the one Cooper gives me. Something about that makes my heart trip all over itself. Could I picture myself married to Cooper one day? Pregnant with his child?

"Sienna, how did you get into baking?" Luna asks, saving me from traveling down a dangerous path.

"My Grams. Taught me everything I know."

"Aw, that's so sweet! Does she love your bakery?" Luna asks excitedly.

"She passed away a while ago," I say, sipping my water to try and swallow down the lump in my throat. Cooper squeezes my leg under the table in a reassuring gesture.

"Oh my gosh, I'm so sorry. My mom died a few years ago. I don't know your whole story, but I can tell that loss was hard for you. I think I recognized your pain that first time we met."

"Yeah," I croak out, feeling exposed and awkward and unable to handle the attention and kindness from an almost stranger.

"But you have Cooper now, and us. Welcome to the family!" She reaches her hand out to squeeze mine and it's too much. All of it.

I slip my hand from hers and dip my head down so my hair shields me from the overwhelming attention.

"Excuse me," I mumble before abruptly scooting my chair out and dashing towards the restrooms.

I barely make it inside the single-stall room before I start hyperventilating. It's like I'm on sensory overload, the lights are too bright, the hum of the other patrons' conversation is too loud, even though it's muffled by the bathroom door. And the kindness. It's too much. Why do these people care about me? I'm nothing. I'm so far below them in every way imaginable. I want to leave. I want to run back to my apartment above the bakery and hide out in my bed for the rest of the day, possibly the rest of my life.

Family.

Luna said family. That word has only ever been empty and painful for me but being with Cooper and experiencing just a little bit of kindness from Luna and Declan has me wanting things, hoping for things that I don't even know how to handle.

I get my breathing under control and splash some cold water on my face, grateful now that I don't have makeup on. Small victories, right? Looking at myself in the mirror, I try to put some walls up. I try to harden my features and force out the weighty feelings of acceptance and hope. Those are dangerous things to get used to.

Except, I find that I can't quite get to that place of indifference anymore. It's like once Cooper invaded my heart and soul, I can't go back to the cold, prickly persona. No, that can't be right. I have to reach for it, have to protect myself, have to stop the flood of emotions welling up and threatening to choke me.

"Goddamnit!" I tell my reflection. "You're stronger than this. You don't need a family, you're fine on your own." My voice cracks on the last word, but my gaze is fierce. I hate feeling weak. I just have to keep it together a little bit longer.

With a final deep breath, I steel myself for the rest of this lunch.

I open the door and run right into Cooper, who appears to have been standing outside the bathroom the whole time. I should walk out. I can't deal with this, with *him* right now. But I stand there and let him press me against the wall of the hallway. I let him brush my cheeks with his fingertips and tangle them in my long hair so he can turn my face up towards his. I let him bend down and kiss me so sweetly, so reverently, my heart aches.

"You deserve to be loved, baby," he whispers into my lips before kissing me again. "You deserve a family. You belong, right here with us. With me."

"How..." I can't even express my thoughts. How the hell did he reach into my head and rip out all of my insecurities and address them one by one?

"I know you, sweetness. You have my heart, which means I can feel when you're hurting. When you're scared. When you're about to run."

I squeeze my eyes shut and fight off a sob. It's too intense, his confession. I want to hide but I also want him to rip me open even more and tell me I'm going to be okay despite all of my flaws and doubts.

He kisses my forehead, my closed eyes, my nose.

"Cooper..." I whisper. I don't even know what I want to say to him, what I need.

He just tucks me into his chest and wraps his arms around me like he knows he's the only thing keeping me together. I find that right here, in this moment, I don't need all of my defenses. Cooper is covering me, protecting me, filling in those empty spaces I've tried to ignore for so long.

"I've got you, kitten," he says softly. "You're safe, baby girl. You're safe with me."

Damn if his words don't make tears sting my eyes as he just holds me and lets me have this moment.

After a few minutes, or hours, who knows, he finally leans back and kisses me on the nose. "Let's get out of here, yeah? Go back home?"

I nod against his chest. I fight the urge to correct him. We're going to *his* home. But I can pretend for a little while that it's mine too.

Chapter 8

Cooper

Sienna is a beautiful mess. She was all over the place yesterday, both from signing her business over and the lunch with Luna and Declan. I had known she was lonely before, from the way she melted into my touch like no one had gotten that close to her in years, but I didn't know the depth of her isolation until Luna showed her genuine kindness.

I saw when it all hit her. I fucking felt it when she tensed and curled up into herself. I knew she wanted to hide, to run, to throw away everything we've been working towards since the day we met. But no way would I let that happen.

After we left the restaurant yesterday, Sienna and I spent the afternoon alternating between going over details of her handing off her bakery and snuggling up on the couch watching bad tv. Turns out my kitten likes sappy romance movies, which pleases me to no end.

She let me pick what to watch first, some action movie. But when I headed off to the shower, Sienna switched the channel and was all curled up making puppy dog eyes at the couple kissing on the screen. It brought a stupid-happy grin to my face to know she secretly wants that in her life. I have no problem providing her a happily ever after.

When it came time for bed, I wanted nothing more than to haul her off to my room, and honestly, I think she would have let me. But it was an emotional day for her, and I knew if I had her warm body pressed against mine all night, I'd have given in to temptation and taken her right then and there.

So, instead of ravishing and worshipping her the way she deserves, the way we both want, I led her back to the guest room and then promptly took my second shower of the day, jerking off to thoughts of my kitten showing me her claws in a whole new way.

Today, we're heading over to Mad Batter so Sienna can show me the ropes. After taking a good look at her expenses and profit margins, we decided to cut the operating hours of the shop and focus on the custom orders, which are much more profitable. The bakery will still be open for the morning and lunch rush, but then we'll close down around one-thirty. Sienna will stay at my place and bake her pastries and such in the morning and I'll take them to the shop. Then she can focus on working on the custom orders during the day.

Sienna was concerned about leaving Mandy all alone while there's a possibility of her mom and Derek showing up, so I told her I'd be there every morning. She of course protested, but I finally wore her down. I might have used tickling and a few kisses, but eventually, she saw things my way.

Declan was on board for me spending the mornings in the bakery and the afternoons at the office. Asher, on the other hand, took a little more convincing. In the end, I told him we're all three CEOs and owners of the company, so my telling him of my plans was entirely out of courtesy. He didn't like that but had no way to argue with me. Especially after I hung up on him.

"Are you *sure* this is a good idea?" Sienna asks from the passenger seat of my car.

"Don't you trust me, sweetness?"

She sighs. "I do, you know I do, it's just this is...this is my life, you know? If I don't have the bakery, I'm nothing," she says quietly.

We pull into the small parking lot of the shop and I turn off the engine and look at her. "Baby, you're not nothing, no matter what happens to the shop."

"What am I then?"

I take a deep breath and hold her gaze, wanting her to hear me, *really* hear me. "You're mine, Sienna."

Her eyebrows shoot up her forehead as her eyes go wide. I can tell she's contemplating what I just said, weighing each word and seeking the truth behind it.

"Why aren't I upset with that? I should tell you I'm not yours to possess, but I..."

"You want to be mine. You trust me to take care of you, not to treat you like an object, but a treasure."

Sienna blinks away tears and nods her head. I give her a tender kiss and then nip at her lips. She giggles, a sound I'll never get tired of, and swats my chest.

"Come on, let's get inside before you distract me even more with your smooth talk and sweet kisses," she says, feigning annoyance.

Sienna starts to open the car door, but I grab her wrist and tug her into me for a passionate kiss. "First of all, kitten, it's not smooth talk," I tell her once we break apart. "I mean every fucking word I say and I'll tell you all the damn time how much you mean to me, how precious and beautiful and *mine* you are." I nip and kiss down her neck, making her gasp and fist the sides of my coat. "And second of all," I growl into the side of her neck, "My kisses aren't always sweet."

I seal my declaration with a rough, possessive kiss. One that has her moaning into my mouth and pulling me closer to her. I fucking devour her lips, her tongue, her entire being. And she gives it right back to me. I can taste the same intensity, the same longing with each stroke of her tongue against mine.

With much self-control and even more regret, I pull my lips from hers. We can't get caught up like this right here when she's at risk. I don't like her being around the bakery for any amount of time, though I know her showing me the ropes is necessary.

Sienna gasps for air, her lips swollen from our kiss, her cheeks rosy red. I can't help but imagine what she looks like when she cums. Fuck, I want to see it, feel it, smell it. I take a deep breath and try to calm the hell down before I drive her back to my place, bend her over the couch, and fuck her until she screams my name.

"Thinking dirty thoughts over there?" Sienna asks all breathily.

"When it comes to you, kitten? Always."

She bites her fucking lip and I have to turn away. Jesus, everything she does has me ready to bow down and worship at her altar. This woman has me completely captivated, wrapped around her little finger, and she doesn't even know the power she holds.

I get out of the car and adjust myself in my jeans, willing my cock to go down.

Sienna is by my side in a second, smirking at me like she's pretty pleased with my state of misery. Maybe she does know the power she has over me. Little minx.

"You already know the basics," she says once we're inside. "The register, helping the customers, keeping the lobby clean. You should know about Mr. Harrelson."

"Oh?"

"He's always the first customer in the morning. No doubt he'll be upset that I've been closed for several days. He gets a croissant, warmed in the oven, along with a cup of half decaf, half regular coffee. He also gets the newspaper I have delivered every morning."

"You get the newspaper?"

She nods. "At first it was a mistake. The guy kept delivering it even though I didn't pay for a subscription. Mr. Harrelson always picked it up on his way in and said if I didn't want to read it, he would. Then one morning, the paper didn't show up. He was *not* happy. So, I got a subscription that afternoon. The paper has been coming ever since, and Mr. Harrelson has been a happy camper. Well, a grumpy camper, but an endearing one, at least."

I grin at her. I knew she was a softie underneath her prickly exterior.

"What?" She says.

"Nothing," I smile.

She rolls her eyes and waves me off, heading towards the back of the shop.

"Okay, so over here is the supply closet where I keep..."

I stand behind her and grab her hips, lightly, pulling her close to me, her back to my front.

"What do you keep in here, kitten?" I ask as I nuzzle her neck. I can't help myself. She's a fucking siren and I just want to feel all of her all the damn time.

"Uh... Um, there are cleaning supplies, and..." she gasps as I suck the sensitive spot where her neck and shoulder meet, pulling her skin between my teeth and biting down softly.

"And what?"

"And..."

My thumbs graze the hem of her shirt and then slip barely underneath, stroking the silky soft skin above her hips.

She clears her throat and steps away from me. "And you really need to stop doing that." Sienna glares at me, but I see the playful grin tugging at her lips. She likes it. She likes knowing I can't resist her. But, she's right. I really do need to pay attention. Playtime can come later.

We go over cleaning out the case, mopping and sanitizing the back room, proper handwashing procedure, and how to turn the ovens on and off.

"You know, for a billionaire, you don't seem to have any issues rolling up your sleeves and getting your hands dirty," she comments sassily as I wipe down the bakery case and she supervises.

I turn around and grab her by the waist, tugging her into my chest. I bend down so my lips graze her ear. "You want to see how dirty my hands can get?"

She moans softly. "I shouldn't find your cheesy line so sexy, but everything you do seems to turn me on," she all but whispers, rubbing her body up against mine in the most exquisite torture.

"Fuck," I groan, guiding her backward and lifting her up so she's sitting on the metal prep table.

She loops her arms around my neck and pulls me down for a kiss, widening her legs so I can grind my hard cock against her pussy. One of my hands rests on the small of her back, keeping her hot little body pressed against mine, while the other tangles in her hair, pulling her head back and exposing her neck to me.

I softly bite down on her pulse point and lick away the sting, loving how she gasps and digs her fingernails into my scalp.

"There are so many things I want to do to your sexy fucking body, kitten," I growl into her neck before kissing her there.

"Oh yeah?" She moans, squeezing her thighs around my hips.

"Yeah, but not here." In my second greatest feat of strength today, I pull away from Sienna, getting some much-needed space.

Sienna pouts, fucking *pouts,* which doesn't help the sorry state of my cock. I help her down off the counter and kiss her forehead, looping my arms around her waist and holding her close.

"When I make you cum for the first time, I need to be able to take my time exploring your perfect little pussy. I can't do that here," I tell her. Sienna's eyes are closed and she's still breathing heavily. "Plus, it's probably unsanitary, right?"

This seems to get her attention. Her eyes snap open and go wide as saucers. "Oh my god. You're right. It's against so many health code violations. I can't believe we almost..." Her face goes bright red and she won't look me in the eye.

"You almost what, sweetness? What were we going to do?" I ask, still not letting go of her hips.

She glares at me and tips her chin up. Fucking adorable. "You know what was going to happen."

"Hmm...I don't know if I do. Wanna spell it out for me?" I tease.

"We were going to desecrate my bakery!" She hisses, making me laugh.

"Desecrate? Oh, baby girl, I thought we were going to memorialize this place. Make it the place where we have the best sex of our lives," I tell her, grinning when I see her face turn an even deeper red. Who knew my woman was so shy about these things? I'll break her out of her shell.

"Or the only sex..." She mumbles. I almost don't hear it, but when the words register, my heart stutters in its tracks.

"What did you say?"

"Nothing," she's quick to backtrack, turning her face away from me.

I gently grasp her chin and make her look at me. "Are you telling me I'm going to be your first?" I hold my breath for her answer.

"Presumptuous much?" She snaps back defensively.

"Sienna..."

"Look, it's not a big deal, okay? Don't make it weird." She tries shoving me away, but I hold her close.

"It is a big deal, sweetness. And *when* we're both ready to have sex, I'll take such good care of you. I love that I get to be your first."

I think she's going to lash out again and say something more about being arrogant, but instead, she looks up at me with those beautiful eyes of hers, searching me for truth.

"Yeah?" She whispers.

I nod in confirmation and give her a sweet, reverent kiss before resting my forehead on hers. "Yeah, kitten. First, last, only."

We stay like that, in our little bubble of sweet promises, for a few moments. Then she pushes back on my chest and looks up at me with a gleam in her eye. "You better make it good if you're expecting me to stick around forever," she smirks.

And just like that, I go from tender protector to savage beast. I spin Sienna around so her back is to my front. My hands dig into her hips, grinding her juicy little ass against my aching cock. I pull her earlobe through my teeth and grin when she tries to hold in her moan. I slide one hand from her hip down to her inner thigh, then up, up, up, until I can feel the heat of her pussy through her yoga pants.

Fuck, I can feel her wetness seeping through the fabric. I cup her mound and rub my fingers back and forth, loving the way her hips automatically grind down on my hand.

"Believe me, sweetness, when I get inside of that perfect pussy of yours, I'm going to fuck you so goddamn deep you'll never forget who you belong to," I growl. "I'll make you scream, make you beg, make you cum so hard, so often, that you won't have time to look elsewhere for satisfaction. I'm going to be your whole world, just like you're already mine."

"Oh god..." She gasps, leaning back into my chest and reaching behind her to tangle her fingers in my hair. I nibble on her neck and slip my hand inside her pants and panties, groaning when she shudders and whimpers at my touch. "Please," she gasps, bucking her hips, trying to get me where she wants me.

I dip one finger into her soaking wet slit, making us both moan. Jesus, her silky little cunt feels incredible. I draw furious circles around her clit, working her up to a frenzy. Sienna gushes for me, trembles in my hands, whimpers my name. I feel her orgasm, close, so close, almost there...

I withdraw my hand, growling as I lick my fingers clean.

"NO! What? Why?" She cries, panting and frustrated, her arms dropping back to her side.

"Good things come to those who wait," I murmur into her neck before nipping the skin there.

Sienna spins around and lets out an angry little growl that makes my dick twitch. She grabs a rag from the sanitizer bucket and wipes down the area she was just sitting on.

"You better go wash and dry your *dirty* hands there, mister," she says, looking at me over her shoulder, trying to be angry failing miserably.

"You got it, *boss*," I grin.

She rolls her eyes but grins back at me.

"Shouldn't I be calling *you* that?"

"That's an interesting element to add to all of this," I tease.

"Oh my *god*, seriously, just wash your damn hands!"

I laugh and swat her on the ass, making her squeal.

Chapter 9

After the longest, most sexually frustrating car ride of my life, Sienna and I are back in the penthouse, sitting on the couch and trying to decide what to have for lunch.

"Indian?" I suggest.

"Nope."

"Chinese?" I try again.

"Nuh-uh."

"A burger?"

"No," she sighs.

"Italian? Sushi? Gyros? Whatever you want, I can get it delivered."

"What if I want you?"

"Fuck, woman," I groan. "I thought we decided we weren't ready for that."

"But what if we do...*other* things?"

"Sienna..." I say in a warning voice. She thinks I'm strong. But she's dead fucking wrong. I'm about to break.

"Well, it's your fault you got me all worked up and then, and then, and you just...*stopped*!" She throws her hands up in frustration.

I'm on her in the next breath, flipping her on her back, pinning her arms above her head and nudging her legs apart.

"You want me to finish what I started, kitten?"

She nods, her pupils dilating and cheeks flushing. So beautiful. "Please, I need it," she breathes out.

I grunt and slam my mouth down over hers, swallowing her moans of pleasure as I thrust my tongue in and out of her sweet lips. Sienna wriggles underneath me and I release her arms, freeing up both of my hands to roam over her body. We break apart, gasping for air, and I get off the couch.

"You've got to be fucking kidding m—"

I cut off her rant by scooping her up in my arms and running towards my bedroom. She gasps and then leans into me, kissing my neck the whole way there.

I set her down and peel off her shirt, letting my hands run up and down the smooth skin of her tummy, her ribs, and then cupping her perfect breasts still covered in a lace bra. I rub my thumbs over her already hard nipples, making her moan and arch her back. I deftly unhook her bra and slide it down her arms before bending down and sucking one perky tit into my mouth.

"Oh fuck," she whispers almost in surprise like she didn't think it would feel this good.

I smile with a mouthful of her breast and bite down gently on her nipple. Sienna's whole body jerks, making me completely ravenous for her.

"Love how responsive you are, kitten," I mumble into her chest before licking and sucking her other breast.

Back and forth I suck, lick, nibble, and knead her tender flesh, and she loves every second. I think I could make her cum just like this, but I have other plans for her. I pop off her tit, making her whimper and pout. Grinning, I drop to my knees in front of her and hook my thumbs into the waistband of her yoga pants.

"This okay, sweetness?"

"Please…" she breathes out.

"Please, what?" I ask, already peppering kisses down her tummy.

"Please, um…lick me?"

I chuckle. "Is that a question?"

"Lick me," she says more confidently.

I grin and lick her tiny tummy, dipping my tongue into her belly button and making her suck in air.

"That's not what I meant," she says, trying and failing to sound annoyed.

"No? Where do you want me to lick you?"

"My...my pussy," she whispers.

I grunt in approval and start tugging her pants and panties down, slowly revealing the curve of her hips. "Why didn't you say so, sweetness?" I ask with my eyes pinned to what is going to be revealed next.

She takes a breath like she's going to say something sassy in response, but then I pull her pants all the way down, baring her ripe, juicy cunt to me for the first time. I help her step out of her clothes and then take my time looking her up and down from my position on my knees in front of her.

My kitten is fucking gorgeous. Too beautiful for words. Too damn beautiful for me, that's for sure. But she's mine anyway and I'm not giving her back. Sienna chews on her lip nervously and I realize I've just been drooling over her flawless skin and succulent curves.

"Sienna..." I whisper in awe. "You're...fuck, baby, you're perfect."

Her brow furrows and she opens her mouth to voice her disagreement, no doubt. She must see something in my eyes that stop those words from coming out of her mouth. Instead, she spears her fingers in my hair and digs her nails into my scalp.

"I want to see you too," she purrs.

"Jesus, I'm trying to be good," I growl.

"And I'm trying to be bad," she retorts.

"Don't tease me, little girl," I warn.

"I...I just want to see you. All of you." Her tone is less seductive siren and more innocent request. "Please?" She adds, sounding a touch insecure now.

I don't say anything, just stand up and pull my shirt over my head. She immediately touches my bare chest, her fingertips tracing my tattoos, followed by her tongue. I growl when she scrapes her teeth over my nipple. Then her hands move lower, roaming over my ribs, the defined muscles of my abs, my lower stomach...

"Fuuuuck," I groan as Sienna palms my cock through my jeans.

"Can I?" She asks, looking up at me with such sincere eyes. Jesus, I could cum from that sight alone.

I nod as she works on my button and zipper, and I help her tug them down my legs. Her eyes go wide when she sees my cock for the first time, and then her hand wraps around my hard length.

"Oh fuck," we both say at the same time. I'd laugh, but I'm concentrating on not nutting in her damn hand right now.

"Now what?" She asks, sliding her hand up and down my shaft, spreading precum as she goes.

"Jesus," I grunt. "Now you have to stop touching me before I lose my fucking mind and tear into you like a goddamn animal."

I worry that I scared her for a second, but she looks at my dick and licks her lips. It jerks in her hand and she gasps, clenching her fist around me. I decide to take control of this situation before the last thread of my sanity snaps.

I fist her hair and tug, giving me access to her sexy mouth. My lips crash down on hers and we lose ourselves in each other's passion. I kick my pants off from around my ankles and walk us towards the bed, giving her a little push. Sienna giggles when her back hits the sheets. I stand in front of her and memorize every line and contour of her perfect body.

"Cooper!" Sienna says, her tone indicating she's been saying my name for a little while now. I can't help it; I'm just so lost in her.

"Yeah, sweetness?"

"Weren't you about to do something?" She smirks.

"I was, but then you changed the game by making me strip down."

She bites her lips and shrugs. "Sorry, not sorry."

God, she's so fucking sexy. "You still want me to lick your sweet pussy?"

Her eyes go dark and she nods, hungrily.

"Then touch yourself."

"Wh-what?"

"You heard me, baby girl. Spread those legs and show me how you get yourself off."

Sienna's face blushes bright red but she lifts her heels to the edge of the bed and opens herself up to me. One little hand snakes down her body and drifts lazily to her glistening, pink pussy. Slowly, so fucking slowly, she dips two fingers into her slit and circles her bundle of nerves.

She gasps as her hips jerk, but she keeps on rubbing her clit and moaning. I take myself in my hand, because how can I not when the most gorgeous woman I've ever seen is sprawled out naked on my bed, touching herself?

When her other hand squeezes her tit, I just about lose it. I have to pinch the tip of my cock to stave off my orgasm. No way in hell am I coming before she does. Ever.

"Enough," I grunt, gently batting her hand away from her pussy. I replace her fingers with mine, circling, circling, circling her little button. "Do you ever put your fingers in here?" I ask as I slide my fingers down to her tight little channel.

She shakes her head no.

"Fuck, are you saying I'll get that honor too?"

"Please," she whimpers.

I don't have it in me to draw this out any longer. I've been teasing myself as well as her all day, and I need to see her cum right the fuck now. Kneeling in front of her, I throw her legs over my shoulders and dive into that pussy. I flatten my tongue and lick from her entrance up to her clit. As soon as I tap her tight bundle of nerves, Sienna erupts.

"FUCK!" She screams, her thighs clamping down on my head, her back bowed off the mattress, her fingers clawing the sheets as her orgasm rips through her.

I don't stop. Not for a second.

Using my tongue, my lips, my teeth, I keep stimulating her throbbing clit, pushing her past her orgasm, higher, higher, higher till she's shaking, gasping for air, pleading me to give her mercy. Only then do I ease off her over-sensitive bundle of nerves and turn my attention to lapping up her release as it drips down towards her cute little ass hole.

Sienna shudders as I gently bring her down with long, steady strokes of my tongue, licking her perfect pussy clean.

I place her legs back on the bed and crawl on top of her, holding myself up with a forearm on either side of her head. I stare down at my girl as she opens her eyes and looks at me with such awe. I can't explain what that does to me. I've never felt anything like it, having her admiration, seeing her like this, knowing I put that look there.

"More," she whispers while rocking her hips and gliding her pussy up and down the underside of my aching cock.

This is dangerous. I know that. I should get off of her. I should put my damn pants on and order some lunch while she gets dressed. But I can't seem to move. I crave her, fucking need her skin on my skin, her taste in my mouth, her breath on my lips. But she's not ready for sex yet, even if she thinks she is right now in her post-orgasmic bliss.

"Please," Sienna whimpers, opening her legs even wider.

"Kitten..."

She cuts me off by leaning up and capturing my lips in a scorching kiss. I growl into her mouth and take over, reminding her who is in control. I take over her movements, sliding my dick up and down her wet pussy, but never entering her. She submits so beautifully to me, trusting me with her body, her pleasure. Back and forth I rub my swollen fucking cock over her sensitive bundle of nerves until she's panting again.

"I need to cum," I tell her.

"Yes, please," she begs, greedy for my seed.

"Cum with me," I demand as I lower myself down onto her, gasping when I feel her hard little nipples scrape against my chest.

"I can't," she whispers. "I'm...it's too much."

"You can," I tell her. "I promise you, you can. And you will. Cum for me again, sweetness."

I rub, back and forth, my dick pinned between my stomach and her pussy, grinding hard, gritting my teeth against the urge to spear her tight little virgin cunt and claim her once and for all. This isn't about that.

I rest my forehead on hers, breathing in her sugary, spicy scent, mixed with our lust. It's intoxicating.

"Cum for me, baby girl, I need you to cum," I half beg, half growl.

And then she does. Fuck, does she cum. Hard.

My kitten shows me her claws, ripping up my back and mewling for me as I try to hold on as long as I can. It feels too incredible, but I need relief. I push myself up on one hand and grab my dick, pumping it twice and then painting Sienna's thighs, pussy, and stomach with the orgasm I've been holding back all day.

"Yes!" She moans, putting her hand over mine and stroking my cock with me.

"Goddamn, such a dirty fucking girl," I growl as we pump the last of my seed from my balls. Sienna drops her hand down to her stomach and rubs my release into her skin, which makes me half-hard all over again.

I groan and lean down for a kiss, knowing if I keep watching her, I'll become fully hard and need to bury my thick cock deep in her juicy cunt.

She sighs into the kiss and then I feel her body go limp beneath me. Rolling to the side, I pull her tiny body into mine and wrap her up in my arms. Sienna shakes slightly against my chest, so I lean back to look her in the eyes.

"You okay, kitten?"

She sighs and then smiles up at me, making my heart squeeze up tightly in my chest, hardly able to contain the emotion that look elicits.

"That was incredible," she says in awe.

"*You're* incredible, sweetness. And *that* was just the beginning," I wink.

"I don't think I can cum any harder than I just did."

"Is that a challenge?" I quirk an eyebrow up at her.

"And if it is?" She smirks.

I growl and kiss her playfully, nipping her lips, and tickling her tummy. Sienna giggles and shrieks, making me laugh along with her. I've never seen her this relaxed, this open, this full of life. I vow to give her multiple orgasms every day if this is the end result.

Chapter 10

Sienna

I'm sitting on the couch now, waiting for Cooper to join me after his shower. He went into the office this afternoon and brought dinner home. I'm impressed that he could focus enough to work, let alone move his body after what we did earlier today.

Closing my eyes, I picture what it was like to have him on top of me, the weight of his body resting on mine, the sound of his grunts in my ear, all of it. God, it was incredible.

"You okay there, kitten?" Cooper's voice filters through my fantasy.

I pop my eyes open and see him leaning in the doorway to the living room.

"Yeah," I say, my voice breathy and husky and giving away far too much.

Cooper quirks an eyebrow up, noticing my tone. "Thinking impure thoughts, are we?"

"Just remembering earlier today," I smile up at him innocently.

His eyes darken and I know he knows what I'm talking about. "Ah, so not impure thoughts," he says, stalking towards me. "Dirty thoughts," he says once he gets to the couch, caging me in with one strong arm on either side of me. "Fucking filthy thoughts," he growls.

And then he kisses me.

No, kissing isn't a strong enough word for what's happening. Cooper is ravishing me, consuming me with his teeth, his tongue, his devil lips. I feel the couch cushion press down with the weight of his knee next to me as Cooper towers over me and tilts my head up by tugging my hair back. He presses me into the couch and places open-mouthed kisses down my neck while I gasp for air.

"Fuck," he finally says, resting his forehead on mine. "You completely unravel me with one look, sweetness. How is that even possible?"

"I don't know, but you do the same thing to me," I tell him honestly. He kisses me once more, then pushes himself off of the couch.

"Alright, now that you've got me all worked up, I'm going to head to bed. I have to be up bright and early for my first day on the new job," he says.

I smile and follow Cooper down the hall but stop when I get to his bedroom door. When he realizes I'm not following him to the guest room I've been sleeping in, he turns around.

"Do you think maybe I could...stay in here with you tonight?" I ask. "I mean, we've already seen each other naked," I shrug, hoping to not make a big deal about it.

Cooper walks back towards me and cups my face in his hands. "Sienna, I want you in there with me, baby, I do. But I want to respect your space and I want to keep my promise to wait until we're both ready to have sex. I don't know if I can control myself with your sexy little body next to me all night long."

I nod and try not to let it hurt. I get it. I really do. And some part of me admires him for wanting to be noble and wait until I'm ready to take things to the next level. But I wasn't even thinking about that. Okay, so I'm *always* thinking about that when I'm around Cooper, but I really just wanted to be in his arms.

"You're right," I tell him, trying to sound casual.

"Baby, please don't be upset."

"I'm not. I'm good. It was just an idea," I shrug.

Cooper frowns, so I give him a chaste kiss and withdraw from his embrace before sauntering down the hall towards my room. "See you at four-thirty in the morning!" I call out.

He gives me a half pained, half teasing groan at the mention of his new wakeup time.

I crawl into bed and try to get some sleep. Like almost every other night since I left my mom and Derek, dark thoughts and worries plague me, making me toss and turn. I feel a nightmare coming on, so I try to stay awake as long as possible.

I don't know how much time as gone by, but I'm in that weird half-asleep, half-awake state when my bedroom door opens. I think for a second I'm imagining it, that soon I'll have a very dirty dream about Cooper, but then I feel the bed dip down with his weight as he crawls in next to me.

Cooper doesn't say anything, he just turns me on my side, facing away from him, and curls his big, warm body around me, pulling my back into his chest.

"I should have let you stay. I'm sorry, kitten," he whispers before kissing the back of my neck. "I couldn't sleep without you in my arms."

Tears burn in my eyes at his admission, but I refuse to let them fall. It's like he once again sees right into my head and speaks directly to my fears and deepest needs. I nod and snuggle deeper into him.

"This is all I wanted," I say softly.

Cooper squeezes me tightly and kisses between my shoulder blades before resting his forehead there. I finally feel myself relax enough to drift off to sleep.

***

Cooper and I have a little routine now. It's been five days of me running the business from the safety of his kitchen, and him working the bakery floor in my stead. We both get up bright and early and Cooper gets coffee going and then helps me whip up the pastries. We sip coffee and have breakfast while everything bakes, and then we load up a van Cooper bought for the business (despite my many protests).

Now I'm working on my second custom order – a cake for a fiftieth wedding anniversary. I can't help but think about Cooper and me, and if we have what it takes to last that long. As much as I love my cheesy romance movies, I honestly never thought I'd have anything like that in my life.

But Cooper came along and threw my whole world out of order. I know I love him. It hit me square in the chest that first morning we woke up together. We shifted throughout the night so I was facing him with one leg wedged in between his. Cooper looked so peaceful, utterly fulfilled, and content to have me in his arms. The alarm was about to go off, so I turned in his arms to grab my phone. Cooper mumbled something and pulled me back, tucking me into his side. I don't think he even knew he was doing it, but something about that simple gesture broke through the last of my reserves.

Since then, we've slept together every night, but it's always just that – sleep. We've made-out a lot, and he's given me several orgasms, but he hasn't gotten naked in front of me again, try as I might to convince him otherwise.

Well, no more. I have a plan for when he gets home, hopefully in the next thirty minutes or so. Something to prove to him that I'm all in and I'm ready for everything he has to give me.

As if sensing my urgency (and horniness), the elevator to his private penthouse dings, and Cooper walks into the kitchen a few seconds later.

"You're early," I say with a bright smile, looking up from the cupcake I'm frosting.

"I couldn't stay away from you any longer," he says, pulling me into his arms.

Untangling myself from his embrace, Cooper pouts, which makes me giggle.

"I have to put the finishing touches on this," I explain, turning towards my cupcakes and giving him my back.

He steps up behind me and winds his arms around my waist, kissing up and down my neck, just like I knew he would. The man can't keep his hands off me. Not that I'm any better. He's so busy nipping and kissing and grinding into me, he doesn't notice when I swipe my finger through the bowl of frosting, gathering up a pretty good-sized scoop of sugary goodness. When I feel his dick getting hard and pressing into my ass, I turn in his arms and welcome his kiss.

Cooper tilts his head to deepen our kiss, and I raise my hand up towards his face. He grabs my wrist right before I get a chance to wipe the frosting on his cheek. Breaking our kiss, he chuckles before sucking the frosting off my finger.

"Ah, you've already tried unsuccessfully to get me with frosting that way, kitten."

I pout, but only so he thinks he's got the upper hand. Right before he goes in for another kiss, I take the cupcake I have in my other hand and wipe it down his neck. Cooper freezes. His face is absolutely priceless.

"Why, you—"

I cut him off by licking the frosting from his neck and quickly unbuttoning his shirt before he can stop me. I kiss and lick down his exposed chest while exploring his abs and back muscles with my hands once I've got his shirt open.

"Sienna..." he groans. "What are you doing to me?"

I look up at him and smirk. "Whatever I want."

With that, I slide his shirt down his powerful shoulders and dip my finger in the bowl of frosting once again. This time he doesn't stop me when I trail a line starting at his sternum and ending right above his belly button.

I flatten my tongue against his hard stomach and lick up towards his chest, never breaking eye contact.

"Fuck," he grunts before winding his fingers in my hair and tipping my head back so he can devour me.

I feel his hands grip the hem of my t-shirt and I lift my arms up so he can take it off. He growls in approval at my choice not to wear a bra. Finally getting in on the game, Cooper dips his fingers in frosting and circles one nipple and then the other. I shiver at the cool cream and then moan when he sucks it off of me.

"Is this what you wanted, my sexy little kitten? You want to drive me fucking crazy?"

"I was hoping to seduce you," I breathe out, my voice caught in my throat as he sucks on my other breast and bites my nipple.

Cooper stops in his tracks and looks at me. "You've been seducing me since the very first moment I held you in my arms, sweetness."

"Well, then how about I finish the job tonight?"

Before he can say anything else, I reach for his pants and get his belt undone.

"Are you sure, Sienna?" He asks, his voice tight with restraint.

I loop my fingers in the waistband of his pants and tug him closer to me while looking up at him.

"I'm sure, Cooper. I want everything with you, and I want it starting tonight."

His eyes somehow manage to go soft and yet sharp with arousal at the same time.

"Thank fuck," he growls. "I can't stay away from you anymore, baby."

"Then don't."

I hardly get the words out of my mouth before Cooper slides my shorts down my legs.

"Damn, kitten. You weren't wearing panties or a bra all day today?" He asks while kneeling in front of me and massaging up my legs.

I shrug and smile down at him.

"Dirty girl," he grunts, kissing a trail from my belly button to the top of my pussy.

In one swift move, Cooper stands up with me in his arms and deposits me on the counter. He stands between my legs and kisses me urgently. When we break apart, I see a playful gleam in his eyes.

"You don't know what kind of game you've started, sweetness," he says, his voice low and gravelly and sexy as fuck.

"Show me then," I reply.

Cooper gathers up some frosting on his fingers and trails a lazy path between my breasts, down to circle my belly button. He lifts his fingers to my mouth and I suck the remnants of the sugary frosting off of his digits, swirling my tongue and nipping the pads of his fingers. I love watching his pupils dilate with every swipe of my tongue. I can't wait until I can taste his cock.

He withdraws his fingers from my mouth and leans in to pull my bottom lip between his teeth. He peppers hungry nips and bites down my neck, my collarbone, and then begins cleaning up the trail of frosting with his tongue. I lean back with my hands behind me on the counter to give him better access. I swear I can feel every swipe of his tongue on my clit.

When he's done, Cooper stands up and guides me so I'm lying down on the counter all the way, and then sets my heels right on the edge, opening my legs wide for him to see all of me.

"Fucking beautiful," he whispers more to himself than to me. His hands are all over me then, cupping my breasts, tickling down my curves, squeezing my thighs.

Cooper kneels down so his face is right in front of my pussy. I close my eyes when I feel his warm breath across my wet opening, and gasp when I feel cool frosting coating my folds. Before I can even process the different sensations, Cooper eats up the frosting, using every part of his mouth on my soft, tender skin.

He growls into my cunt and nips at my clit, making my inner muscles contract and my legs snap around his head. I feel Cooper's tongue circle around my tight little hole and slowly push inside of me for the first time.

"Oh!" I yelp, the unfamiliar sensation quickly giving way to absolute pleasure. His wicked tongue darts in and out of me and then circles my clit, again and again, working me up into a frenzy.

I hold my breath as the muscles in my back all tense up. I buck my hips and moan every time Cooper's tongue hits me just right, sending jolts of electricity through my body. Slowly, one finger slides into my cunt, and I squeeze around it tightly, making Cooper groan.

"Jesus, you're so tight. It's going to feel fucking incredible to be inside of you, sweetness."

He keeps pumping his finger in and out of me while sucking on my clit. Then there are two fingers stretching my tight channel, and with a sudden flick of his wrist, Cooper hits some spot inside of my cunt that has my orgasm slamming into me, my entire body curling in and then exploding with uncontrollable waves of pleasure, so intense I can't breathe.

Cooper doesn't stop, he doesn't let up for one second, he just licks me right through it, pushing my orgasm beyond anything I've experienced so far. His ruthless tongue drags across my tender flesh, lapping at my release. He growls and sucks on my pussy making wet, sloppy noises. The man is an animal, gorging on my cunt, making me pant and moan and grab his head, shoving it deeper into me. I can't get enough. Neither can he.

I cum again around his fingers, bowing my back off the counter. Cooper grunts into my still-convulsing pussy and guides my legs over his shoulders. His hands slip underneath my ass and bring me impossibly closer to his mouth so he can lick me clean. My bones are liquid by the time he's done.

I'm vaguely aware of being lifted up in Cooper's arms and carried into his room. When he sets me down, Cooper kisses my forehead, nose, and lips so sweetly. He cups my cheeks and rests his forehead on mine.

"Are you sure about this, kitten?"

I nod and place my hands on the outsides of his, looking into those kind, blue eyes of his that have so quickly become my home. "I trust you, Cooper. I want you. I can't wait any longer.

"I know, baby," he says, kissing me deeply, brutally, and yet reverently. "I'm gonna make you feel so good, I promise," he whispers into the side of my neck before kissing me there. Cooper skims his hands down my body and walks us towards the bed, where he gently pushes me down so I'm spread out before him.

Seeing the way his body reacts to mine, the way his gaze darkens, how his cock hardens even more in the confines of his pants, makes me feel sexy and confident. I spread my legs wide and offer myself to him.

"Jesus," he grunts, ridding himself of the rest of his clothing. "So goddamn gorgeous. My beautiful, sexy sweetness giving me her delicious body..."

Cooper stands in front of me completely naked, and god, how I've missed looking at all of him. Feeling all of him. I sit up and reach out for his thick dick, but he catches my wrist and pulls it away.

"I'm afraid you've got me right on the edge, kitten. I swear if you breathe on me I'm going to cum, and I want this to last longer than that."

"Oh..." I blush, not sure what to say to that. "So...now what?" I wince at my own ignorance, but Cooper cups my face and traces his thumb over my jaw.

"Now you let me enjoy you. Let me have control, kitten. Let me make your first time incredible."

I nod and lean back on the bed, opening myself up again for him. Cooper takes another moment to look me up and down. I feel the heat of his gaze over my skin, my nipples, my lips, and then he locks his eyes on mine.

Never breaking eye contact, Cooper crawls on top of me and settles between my legs, rubbing his cock up and down my slit while resting his weight on his forearm beside my head.

"Ready?" He asks.

I nod and squeeze my eyes shut, preparing for the pain of losing my virginity.

"Hey, look at me, Sienna," Cooper says so softly.

I open my eyes and see Cooper looking at me with such longing, such desire, but beyond that, I see the kindness and patience of the man I love. "I'm ready," I whisper.

He kisses me sweetly and lines himself up with my entrance. I feel the head of his cock stretching me wide open, and he's hardly even inside of me yet. I tense up and hold my breath. Cooper stops and nuzzles the side of my neck.

"Breathe, sweetness," he whispers in my ear. "I promise I'll take good care of you."

I take a deep breath and turn my head to kiss him while he surges forward, stretching me with his massive cock. Cooper works his length inside of me one shallow thrust at a time until he bumps up against my barrier.

"Look at me, kitten. I want to see you the second I make you mine forever." His voice is shaking, his muscles tense with the effort of holding back.

"Do it, Cooper. Make me yours."

He pulls back slightly and then thrusts inside of me all the way. I cry out and cling to him as he splits my body open.

"I'm sorry, baby girl. You're doing so good. Are you okay?" His tone is equal parts concern on my behalf and pained that he can't move. I'm struck again at the self-control this man has over his own body all so I can be comfortable.

"I'm okay, Cooper. I'm so...full. It doesn't hurt much anymore."

"Yeah?" He croaks out, resting his forehead on mine.

I wiggle my hips, trying to get used to the feeling of him inside of me. I like it. Not only how he makes my skin light on fire and my pussy throb in ways I couldn't even imagine a few minutes ago, but I like knowing we're as connected, as close as two people can possibly be. I'm already losing track of where I end, and he begins.

"Move, Cooper. I need you to move."

"Fuck," he groans. "I don't want to hurt you, Sienna."

I buck my hips and wrap my legs around him, taking him impossibly deeper. We both cry out with the rush of sensations, and a wave of wetness flows out of me.

"Please," I beg, wiggling my hips again.

He crushes my lips with his and pulls out of me only to push back inside, hitting me deep. Cooper growls and fists my hair, tugging my neck up so he can kiss and bite me there.

"You feel so damn good, sweetness. This pussy was made for me," he grunts while picking up the pace.

I moan when I feel his mouth over my breast, his tongue flicking at one pebbled nipple and then the other. My fingers weave in his hair to hold him to my chest while I arch my back, wanting to feel more of him, all of him.

Cooper slides one hand to the curve of my ass and then squeezes roughly, lifting up my lower half to meet him thrust for thrust. Each time he hits home, my muscles tense and I let out a little whimper. The pleasure feels unreal. My pussy walls flutter, my muscles shake, my eyes burn with the effort of keeping all of these sensations inside of me.

"That's it, Sienna, cum on my big fucking cock," Cooper demands.

I feel my orgasm rising to the surface. It starts deep inside of me, a pinpoint of bright light that trickles throughout my body. Each ragged breath and rough stroke adds to that bright light until my whole being is engulfed in pure energy. Cooper slams into me, shocking my body into an intense orgasm. It feels like my chest is being ripped open as I scream and convulse in his arms.

When I come back down, Cooper kisses my forehead so gently, then nuzzles my neck.

"Can your gorgeous fucking body take any more, kitten?" He asks before pulling my earlobe through his teeth.

"Fuck..." I exhale. "Fuck yes."

Cooper growls and pulls out of me, flipping me on my stomach and pulling my hips back. He squeezes and massages my ass cheeks before pulling them apart and stroking his cock up and down my slit, from my clit all the way to my puckered asshole. I shudder at the thought of him taking me there. I should be scandalized, right? But instead, I'm absolutely *dripping* at the thought. As if reading my mind, Cooper leans over me, his muscled chest covering my back, and kisses between my shoulder blades.

"Not today, sweetness. But soon, I'm going to have every inch of you."

I whimper and nod my head, suddenly feeling empty without him filling me up in some way. "I need you, Cooper," I beg, not even caring if that makes me wanton or weak or slutty. I'll be slutty for him any time.

"Need you too, kitten," he grunts, slapping my ass once and then thrusting all the way inside of me.

"FUCK!" I yell, gasping for air and digging my fingers into the mattress. "Oh fuck, you're so deep, so deep..."

I trail off, unable to complete the thought as Cooper pistons in and out of me, hitting that special spot with each powerful stroke of his fat cock. I press my body back into him, increasing the friction and causing us both to moan.

Cooper slides one arm under my hips to keep me in place while he fucks me savagely. His other hand skims up my back, the soft feeling of his fingertips tickling up my spine intensified by the hard pounding his giving me.

I feel his fingers twist in my hair, pulling my head to the side so he can lean down and kiss me. His abs flex and tense against my lower back as Cooper stuffs me full of his dick and tongue at the same time.

I bite his lip and he snarls into my mouth, making me even wetter for him.

"I want to feel you cum like this," he says in a gravelly whisper before kissing the spot between my neck and shoulder.

Before I can respond, Cooper pinches my clit and bites my shoulder, making my pussy snap almost painfully tight around him.

"God fucking damn, I love feeling you climax on my cock. You're incredible, too fucking incredible."

I think he's going to cum too, but instead, he pulls out and flips me back over, entering me again in one swift motion.

"Cooper!" I scream, coming again, or maybe still. I claw at his back as my body jerks, every movement sparking a deep, insatiable need.

"Sienna," he grunts, holding himself up by one hand beside my head. His other hand grips my hip and steadies my trembling body as he buries his massive dick inside of me again and again, tearing me apart ruthlessly in the best way possible.

Each stroke winds me up, up, up, my pleasure mounting into an almost unbearable orgasm. Everything goes white as my climax ravishes me from the inside out. My back bows, pressing my tits up against Cooper's hard muscles, and then I curl up in his arms, burying my head in his chest right as he roars his own release.

His arms give out and Cooper collapses on top of me, his large, warm body blanketing mine and keeping me sheltered from the storm of emotions and sensations rushing through my body. He tries to roll away, but I cling to him, needing his skin on my skin just a little bit longer.

"I don't want to crush you, sweetness," he chuckles into the side of my neck before kissing me there.

Cooper rolls to the side, but keeps me in his arms, pressing me close to his body. My eyes are closed and I'm still shaking from my multiple orgasms, but Cooper slowly calms me down with the gentle touch of his fingertips swirling over my skin.

When I open my eyes, I floored by the look of awe in his deep blue eyes.

"That was...Jesus, kitten, that was amazing."

I nod and grin at him, giggling when he kisses all over my face. He tucks my hair behind my ear and presses his lips to mine, just savoring our closeness.

We stay like that for a while, on our sides, facing one another. Cooper runs his hand up and down my curves, tracing my outline, drawing me into being, giving me shape and purpose and meaning.

"How are you feeling?" He finally asks, breaking the silence.

"Like I couldn't move even if you paid me a million dollars," I reply.

"Then I did my job right," Cooper grins. "Besides, you don't have to move. I'll be right back."

Before I can protest, Cooper hops out of bed. A few moments later, he is beside me, turning me on my back. I feel a warm washcloth on my inner thigh, and instinctively I grab for it so he doesn't have to do anything else.

"I'm taking care of you, just let me," he says softly before kissing my thigh and resuming his task.

I flinch when he wipes down my pussy, still sore and sensitive from everything.

"Dammit, I'm sorry, sweetness. I was too rough, wasn't I?"

"No, no, I wanted it. You were so good to me, just like you promised." He doesn't look convinced. I cup his cheek and make him look up at me. "Please don't regret this. I know I don't. It was perfect. You were perfect," I reassure him.

Cooper tosses the washcloth towards his bathroom and crawls in bed with me, tucking me into his side.

"I don't regret being with you, baby," he says, playing with my hair. "I could never regret that. I've wanted you for so long. I would never forgive myself if I pushed you too far though."

"Cooper, I don't think anyone has ever had a better first time in the history of the world," I sigh dreamily.

This gets him to smile, finally. We both melt into each other and drift off to sleep.

Chapter 11

Cooper

I slowly wake up, my body tingling with something. A warm, wet sensation on my...

"Sienna?" My eyes snap open to see my beautiful, sexy woman take my hard cock into her mouth. "Oh, baby, what are you doing?" I groan.

She pops off my dick and gives me a sexy smirk. "I thought it was only fair. You made me cum so many times last night, so you deserve a few more orgasms. Plus, it's your day off from the bakery, so I figured we'd make the most of our time." Without waiting for my response, Sienna licks the tip of my cock, wiggling her tongue into the slit on top and making me buck my hips.

Sienna swirls her tongue around the head of my cock and then kisses up and down my length, making me twitch with need. Never has anyone gone down on me like this, like she's worshiping me. As much as I want to slam my dick down her pretty little throat, I can't deny there's something so fulfilling, so perfect about her sweet kisses mixed in with lustful licks.

Finally, she takes me fully into her mouth once again, testing how much of me she can fit. When she gags around my girth, I have to hold myself back from thrusting farther down her throat. She's not ready for that, and this is a precious gift she's giving me right now.

I weave my fingers in her silky black hair and pull her back slightly, helping her find a good rhythm. One of her hands slides up my thigh where she was digging her nails into my flesh in the most delicious way and cups my balls.

I can't help it, my hips snap and let out a primal grunt. Sienna moans around me and speeds up, taking me a little deeper each time. It's too fucking good and I know I'm going to lose it any second.

"Fuck, baby, so damn good," I manage to grit out. I squeeze my eyes shut and grind my teeth together hoping to hold my orgasm off as long as possible. This feels incredible and I don't want it to end.

When I open my eyes again, I see Sienna fingering herself, trembling, with her mouth full of my cock. Jesus fucking Christ it's the sexiest thing I've ever seen.

"I'm gonna cum, sweetness," I growl in warning as I tug on her hair to lift her off of me.

To my absolute shock, she shoves her face down even farther, the head of my cock bumping up against the back of her throat. She moans and swallows me down, making me cum instantly.

"FUCK! Oh fuck, baby, yes," I yell, still coming down her throat.

Sienna sucks down everything I give her and then comes to a shuddering climax herself. She pops off my softening dick and cries out again and again, shaking and still pumping her fingers in and out of her tight little cunt.

Goddamn, my baby is dirty as fuck, and I will never get enough of her.

When she collapses into my lap, I reach down and pull her up my body, slamming my mouth down on hers. She tastes like me, and fuck if that doesn't have my dick roaring to life. We break apart, panting, and Sienna curls up into my side, a satisfied grin on her lips.

"Shit, what a way to wake up," I say. Sienna giggles and kisses my chest.

"So it was okay?"

"Okay? Kitten, that was the best goddamn blow job ever. Jesus, when you came right after me...you're so amazing," I tell her honestly.

She smiles and buries her head in the side of my neck. "I've never done that before, but I saw you there all naked and just had to taste you."

I cup the back of her neck and lift her head up to rest my forehead on hers. "I love that I get to be all of your firsts, Sienna. And you can taste me any time you want," I grin.

"Any time?" She quirks her eyebrow up in challenge.

"Is my sweetness into exhibitionism?"

"I don't know. We should probably try it out sometime and see."

"*Fuuuuck*," I groan, my dick twitching at the thought. I just came not that long ago, but I'm learning that this woman in my arms can have me ready to go in a moment's notice.

I try to think of something else, something less likely to cause me to become fully hard again. I don't know if Sienna is still sore from last night, and I would never hurt her by moving too fast. God, I fucked her so hard and she took every goddamn thrust like the sex queen she is. Shit, this isn't helping.

"Tell me about your tattoos," I say after clearing my throat. I trace the colorful designs with my fingertips, focusing on the beautiful body art instead of...well, her beautiful body.

"The wildflowers are in memory of my Grams," Sienna says softly. It takes me by surprise, considering how her grandma abandoned her, even if the woman eventually left everything to her. "When I was called in for the reading of the will, the first thing her attorney handed me was a handwritten letter from Grams. There was a little bouquet of pressed and dried wildflowers."

"What did the letter say?"

"It was an apology. She said she was sorry for not being more active in my life, that it hurt too much to see her daughter spiral downward. She admitted that wasn't much of an excuse, but she hoped she could provide for me now. There was a quote at the end, something I'll never forget. *Like wildflowers, you must allow yourself to grow in all the places people never thought you would.*"

She has a soft, wistful smile on her face. I bend down and kiss the top of her head, letting her have this quiet moment to remember her grandma.

"My first tattoo was this one," she turns her arm to show me the inside of her forearm, right below the crook of her elbow. I lift her arm and kiss the words. *Be you, bravely.* "As for the rest, I guess they are just little moments I wanted to collect along the way. The skyline of New York the first time I sat on the Brooklyn Bridge, the crazy cartoon mad hatter hat for the bakery, stuff like that. Plus some shit I thought looked cool and tied everything together."

I grin at her attempt to cover up the obvious emotion each tattoo brings up. "They're beautiful, baby," I whisper before kissing her sweetly.

"What about you? You've got more ink than me. Any good stories?"

"Not really. Mostly shit I thought looked cool," I grin down at her, giving her words right back. "My first tattoo, however, was a contest I lost to my brother."

"Oh?"

I shake my head and roll my eyes at the memory. "Declan and Asher and I had a drinking contest. I was convinced I was the young, cool brother, and that I could drink the two of them under the table. Asher thought he had it in the bag since he was the oldest. But Declan surprised the hell out of both of us by playing the slow and steady game. I went hard and fast in the beginning and threw up after an hour. Asher actually passed out not long after. Declan kept drinking and drinking, didn't even get a hangover the next day. Bastard. The deal was the winner got to pick tattoos for the losers."

"And? What did you have to get?"

I lift up my left arm so she can see the inside of my upper arm.

"Tigger?!" She laughs and then covers her mouth with her hand to stifle the sound.

I nod solemnly but can't keep a straight face for long. "Declan said it was the cartoon character that best represented me. Asher's is way worse."

"Ah, so it was not only embarrassing but personal, too. I like Declan's style."

"Hey, you're supposed to be on my side!"

She smirks and shrugs, biting her lip. "How old were you?"

"Seventeen."

"You had a drinking contest when you were seventeen? And how were you able to get a tattoo?"

"Asher got me in, had a fake ID made and everything. He wasn't always the cold, calculating ass he is today."

"I actually don't know much about him. You don't talk about your family other than Declan and Luna. What was your childhood like?"

I nod but don't offer much else. Well, I wanted a distraction from my lust, and bringing up the fam sure did the job.

"You don't have to tell me," Sienna is quick to backtrack.

"No, I want to. I just don't talk about it, like you said. It's nothing all that bad. Poor rich kid and all that."

Sienna props herself up on my chest, locking her eyes on me and holding me captive. It never ceases to amaze me just how fucking beautiful she is. It's unreal.

"I want to know everything about you," she says, her eyes full of compassion that I don't deserve. She's been through so much, and yet she wants to take on my baggage too.

"Dad started White Knight Advertising when he was fresh out of college with some other trust fund babies. The business took off thanks to the right connections and some big-name clients. It was always the understanding that the business was dad's first love, his first baby. At first, the lifestyle of extravagance distracted Declan, Asher, and I from the fact that we would always be second place. Or maybe third place, after mom. She didn't stick around for long, though."

"What do you mean?" Sienna whispers, resting her head on my chest while I rub circles on her back.

"I guess she got tired of being put on the back-burner and basically being a single parent. After having a string of affairs that my dad didn't seem to care about, she left with an eighteen-year-old kid who was set to inherit a fortune. Last I heard they set up shop in the Cayman Islands."

"That's awful," Sienna says, placing a sweet kiss over my heart and then resting her palm there as if to seal it in. "Who raised you after that if your dad was so busy?"

"A mix of nannies and other staff. I think dad did what he could to rally after mom left. Unfortunately, he never really spent time with us before, so he didn't know how to relate to his three kids. He bonded with us the best way he could – grooming us to take over the business. Only, it kind of turned into him pitting us against one another. He could be manipulative and cruel, especially after we all became adults and started working for him."

"Did you ever consider doing something else?"

"Sure, briefly while I was in college. Turns out I really like marketing, specifically researching different strategies and getting on top of trends. I figured I'd spend a few years at White Knight and then maybe branch out and do my own thing. But you know how it goes. I got comfortable, and I think a part of me always felt like Declan and Asher needed someone else to balance out all of their seriousness and tendency to brood. And then dad died almost two years ago now, and he left us all equal shares in the company. I liked the idea of building something bigger than what dad imagined, a legacy we could be proud of, you know? I hoped without dad around, the three of us would be close again like we were when we were kids."

"Are you? Closer?"

"Declan and I have come a long way. I was always closer to him anyway, but he became a bit of a hothead when put under dad's pressure, especially after dad died. But then Luna came along and changed everything. She's really good for him, and I have her to thank for giving me my brother back." I smile at the last few months of getting to know Declan again.

"I'm glad you have that," she says. "What about Asher?"

"Ah, good ol' Ash," I sigh. "I don't know what it's going to take to thaw out his cold, dead heart. I know he took the brunt of dad's twisted games, and yet for how cruel dad was to him, Ash tried harder than any of us to please him. Plus, he's even more messed up about women and relationships than Declan was, so there's that."

"How so?"

"He has all these rules designed to keep everyone at arm's length. He doesn't trust anyone, sometimes not even Declan and me. No relationships, no spending the night with a woman, no inviting women over to his place. Shit like that. Declan was less calculated and purposeful about his standoffishness, but it was there all the same. Distrustful, no attachments, all of that."

"Hmm. But not you?"

"Nah. I mean, I won't lie, when I was younger I was with other women..." I wince just thinking about it. I was never a dick to any of the women I slept with, we both had fun and sometimes we'd hook up again, but I just never found anyone worth settling down with.

"It's okay, Cooper. I figured you had a past. I'm not upset about it."

I let out a breath I didn't know I was holding.

"These last few years though, I wanted something more. I don't know what changed, but I just had this feeling. Shit, I don't know how to explain it. I knew something real was out there. Someone worth holding on to for good, someone I could mean something to."

"You mean everything to me," Sienna says, lifting herself up again so she can kiss me.

Fuck, she's it for me. I knew it the moment I caught her in my arms at Declan's wedding, but the more time I spend with her, trading secrets and sorrows, the more she's woven into the fabric of my being.

"God, Sienna, you mean every-fucking-thing to me," I tell her once we break apart. I watch as her pupils dilate and her breathing grows shallow. I can't help but look at her tits moving up and down with her breath. When I look back up at her, Sienna stares at me with such hunger and passion.

"I need you," she whispers.

"I don't want to hurt you, sweetness. Are you still sore?" She shakes her head no, but I still have my reservations. "Let's take a shower together. The warm water will feel good."

She narrows her eyes at me but then gets a devious look on her face. "You may think you're distracting me from getting your huge dick inside of me, but the joke's on you because I've always wanted to have shower sex."

"Fuck, that's not even fair," I groan. "When did you get such a dirty mouth on you?"

I don't give her a chance to respond, however, before standing up with her in my arms. I kiss her the entire way to the bathroom, only breaking apart so I can start the water. Once it's a good temperature, I guide Sienna inside with me, thankful we're both still naked as can be from the night before. I don't know if I can survive another second without licking every inch of her tight little body.

I watch as the warm water trickles down over her flawless skin and supple curves. My hands follow the droplets of water over her shoulders, her waist, her hips. I grab ahold of her perky ass and pull her towards me, kissing her soundly. She lifts one leg over my hip and I hold it firmly in my grip, groaning at the way she's opening herself up to me.

"Sienna..." I groan into the side of her neck as I kiss my way down her slender column. She thrusts her hips and rubs her hot pussy against my rock fucking hard cock.

"Please?" She whimpers. "I need to feel you. I need…"

I pull back slightly so I can rest my forehead on hers. "What do you need, baby?"

"I need to feel that connection again. It was more than physical. Wasn't it?"

"Damn right it was, sweetness," I say before kissing away all of her doubts and insecurities. My hands roam over her body, stroking, squeezing, savoring every inch.

Finally, I break our kiss and spin her around so she's facing the back wall of the shower. Sienna takes the hint and braces herself on the wall and sticking her ass out, presenting herself to me in an act of complete trust.

"Fuck, kitten, I'll never get used to how gorgeous you are," I mummer before kissing her in between her shoulder blades and ghosting my lips and nose down her spine.

Reaching between her legs, I dip two fingers inside of her wet slit to check her readiness. Goddamn, my kitten wasn't kidding; she needs this.

"Ready for me to fill you up again, sweetness?" I ask while lazily pumping my fingers in and out of her soaking wet hole.

"God, yes, please, please…" Sienna moans.

I stand up behind her and grip her ass, massaging her perfect cheeks and pulling them apart, exposing all of her to my hungry eyes. I lean over and cover her, pressing my chest into her back as I reach around her with one hand. She shivers beneath me. I bite her shoulder, cup her breast, and drive my cock into her mercilessly, letting out a feral growl as I bottom out. She whimpers with each thrust and pushes back into me, letting me know she's right here with me.

I skim fingers down her torso, all the way to her pussy. Her clit is a fat little pearl, swollen and throbbing for me. She bucks against my hand as I play with it, rubbing and pinching and not letting her take a breath as I give her body more pleasure than she's ever known. She twists and cries in agony, but I don't stop. She's mine now. Mine to please. Mine to torture. She arches in my arms as I take her apart piece by piece, letting out a desperate plea right before she breaks.

"That's it, fucking cum for me, Sienna," I grunt, still pumping into her and teasing her nipples with one hand while rubbing her hard little clit.

"Cooper! Fuck!" Sienna gushes for me, her tight pussy spasming around my cock again and again.

I don't let her come back down, I keep drilling her harder and faster, gripping her ass and pulling her cheeks apart.

"Fucking love watching your pussy swallow my big dick," I grunt.

"I... c-can't stop...c-coming..." she gasps in between each word like it's taking up all of her concentration just to breathe.

I wrap one arm around her hips and one across her perfect breasts, holding her up as her knees give out. Sienna is screaming my name and pounding her fist on the wall of the shower as another orgasm is torn from her very depths. Fucking beautiful.

I'm so lost watching her get obliterated by pleasure, that my climax slams into me unexpectedly. I roar as I thrust into her one last time, pressing her trembling body flush against the shower wall. I cum almost violently, jet after jet shooting out of my dick as it swells and spasms inside of her.

Stumbling back a bit, I gather Sienna up in my arms and slowly slide down to the floor of the shower, not trusting my legs at the moment. She curls up into me, still shaking and breathing heavily.

"You okay, kitten?" I ask, still out of breath myself. Goddamn, that was the hardest I've ever cum, the most intense orgasm of my entire life.

"So good," she sighs.

I grin and nuzzle into the top of her head, letting the hot water pour over our bodies and relax our sore muscles. I chuckle softly when I hear Sienna's cute little snores. Poor girl was so exhausted she fell asleep in the shower.

I hold her for a few more minutes, soaking up everything about this moment. Regrettably, I have to wake her up so we can wash up before the water turns cold.

"Sorry, baby," I whisper while gently shaking her awake.

"Hmm?" She slowly blinks her breathtaking eyes open. Her eyes go wide as she realizes she passed out in my arms, and then an adorable blush covers her cheeks. "Oh, wow," she giggles. "I guess I was wrong before."

"About what?"

"I didn't think I could cum any harder, but...you really outdid yourself," she grins up at me.

"You're fucking perfect," I tell her before kissing her. I can't help it. I don't ever want my lips to be away from hers.

I help us stand up and then wash every inch of her before drying her off and putting one of my shirts on her. She rolls her eyes and tells me she can take care of herself, but she secretly likes me taking care of her. I know I do.

Chapter 12

Sienna

It's hard to believe I've been here for two weeks already. Everything feels so natural with Cooper like we've been together for years instead of a few weeks. I feel this incredible connection, this intimacy with him that I never thought I'd experience. Hell, I didn't even think something like this existed.

It's more than our undeniable chemistry, though there's something to be said for that, too. As soon as Cooper walks in the door from work, we're all over each other. He always puts my pleasure first, pushing my boundaries just a little bit, making me cum so hard, so many times, I can't imagine sex with anyone else would even come close to what I feel when I'm with him.

But, like I said, it's more than that. Cooper is this incredibly hard worker, even if he likes to give off the vibe that he's the comic relief. He's kind and selfless and he *knows* me in a profound way that I don't even know myself. As cheesy as it sounds, I truly feel whole with Cooper by my side.

I thought I was content to be alone in my bakery, in my apartment, in my life. As long as I wasn't with my mom, anything felt like a dream come true. Little did I know how much I was missing until Cooper came along and filled my world with joy and love and safety. I've never really known those things, but he reminds me of them every single day.

Sometimes I forget the whole reason I'm staying here. It's been weeks since I got the package from my mom, and Cooper makes me feel so safe and wanted that for the first time in over a year, I'm not looking over my shoulder.

That's probably what gave me the confidence to go out and shop this afternoon. Cooper never specified if he wanted me to stay inside his penthouse twenty-four-seven, but that's just kind of how it's worked up until this point. He has everything anyone could ever need in his place. *More* than anyone could ever need, really. And let's be honest – before I met Cooper, I pretty much just worked and then crashed in front of my TV upstairs until I had to get up and start the day all over again.

Today, however, I want to do something special. Usually, Cooper cooks for us, claiming I baked all day and I need a break. I tried protesting the first few nights, saying he worked two jobs, but he just kissed me senseless and cooked dinner anyway. Well, tonight I'm cooking, no matter what he says. And I'm going to give him another little surprise I hope he likes.

I have the meal all planned out – roasted lamb with garlic and rosemary, cheesy potatoes, and seared asparagus. As for my other surprise...

"*Bienvenue*, how can I help you today?" The gorgeous saleslady greets me in the most elegant French accent.

"Some, uh..." I feel my cheeks pinken with a bit of embarrassment. I'm still so new to this.

"Ah," the saleslady says, giving me a knowing smile. "Lingerie to show off to your lover?"

I nod my head, feeling a little better that she doesn't seem to even bat an eyelash. In fact, she looks pretty pleased that I want to try on the expensive pieces of lace in her French boutique.

We spend the next hour working through different styles, cuts, and colors. I end up with three different pieces, each one more daring than the last. I think Cooper will approve.

Feeling good about my purchases, I walk out of the little boutique and turn left towards the nearest market. One minute I'm strolling down the street, looking at my phone, and the next minute, I'm shoved up against a brick wall in an alley with a cloth pressed against my nose and mouth.

I don't have time to scream or fight back before a sweet chemical smell permeates my nostrils and my vision blurs. The last thing I see is Derek's ugly mug grinning at me, missing teeth and all.

***

"Fuck, how much did you use?"

"I don't know, I don't think there's a limit."

"She's been out for hours, we wanted her incapacitated, not dead. She's no good to us dead."

The voices are garbled and a bit unclear, yet there's a familiar tone to them. My head is throbbing in time to my heartbeat and I feel like I can't quite get a full breath. As my body slowly stirs awake, I become aware of other sensations. The cold floor pressing against my cheek. Something wadded up in my mouth, keeping me from breathing too well. Duct tape stretched across my lips. A searing pain in my shoulder when I try to move, no doubt from when I was dumped on the floor. A zip tie digging into my wrists, which are secured tightly behind my back. I try sitting up, but my stomach rolls as a sudden wave of nausea passes through me.

"Look, she's up. She's fine." I know that voice. Derek.

It all comes back to me. I got too comfortable with Cooper, and now I'm paying the price. Of course, they were always going to find me. Cooper mentioned trying to track my mom and Derek down, but other than a brief update last week telling me he was still working on it, I didn't hear anything on the subject. Again, I got too comfortable living out my fantasy of happily ever after with Cooper. It was always going to come to this, though.

"Daughter of mine," my mom says, squatting down so she can swipe the hair out of my face. I do my best to glare at her, but my blinding headache makes it hard to focus. I do notice, however, that she's wearing a ridiculous ski mask. "You're looking well. Too well. We need to rough you up a bit for this next part."

Her words barely register before she backhands me. It doesn't really hurt so much as it shocks me. It's been a while since she and I went at it. I see her winding up for another, more devastating blow, but my fight or flight instinct kicks in and I roll away from her, landing on my back and screaming when my shoulder pops out of its socket.

"Oh, that's good. Did you get that on camera, hun?"

I tilt my head up to see Derek nodding and holding his phone out, filming our little interaction. I try asking what the fuck they want, but my words get soaked up by the cloth in my mouth and duct tape on my lips.

She lunges at me again, but I swing my legs around and kick at her. I can hardly focus through the pain ripping through my left shoulder as I writhe around on my back, my hands still tied behind me.

"Ah, ah, ah, none of that now, dear." With that, my mom stomps on my right foot with her ridiculous hot pink heels.

I hear the crunch of bone and cartilage before I can register the agonizing pain. I try to be silent since they seem to want to capture my pain on camera, but a whimper escapes. God, I sound so pathetic.

Mom bends down close to me, so close I can smell her familiar scent of menthol cigarettes and drug store perfume. So close I can see the cracks in her caked-on makeup where her wrinkles run deep. So close I can headbutt her. So, I do.

"You fucking bitch!" She screeches, stumbling backward and landing on her ass. The duct tape is preventing my satisfied grin, but it's there nonetheless.

"Switch me," Derek grunts, putting on his own ski mask and handing the phone off to mom.

Well, shit.

He grabs me up by the collar of my shirt into a sitting position, while mom squats down in front of me, getting a clear shot of my face. Derek rips the duct tape off my mouth, replacing it with his hand.

He squeezes my cheeks painfully, forcing the wadded-up cloth in my mouth to the back of my throat and making me gag.

"Listen to me, you worthless cunt," Derek grits out, his putrid breath making me gag all over again. "Tell your boyfriend how much pain you're in, beg him to spare your life. The only way you're getting out of here is if he pays your ransom, so you better make it good."

For the first time since I woke up in this damp and dingy basement, I am afraid. They know about Cooper. They've been following me for a while now. They knew the exact moment I left the penthouse. This attack is much more planned out than I thought it would be. And the stakes are exponentially higher.

I figured they'd find me eventually and I'd be forced to liquidate my assets and hand over whatever I could. Maybe they'd take that and leave, or maybe they'd force me to live with them again and work off the rest of my "debt."

But no. They brought Cooper into this. They're using me to get even more money. I hate myself for putting him in this position after everything he's done for me. I fucking love him and I refuse to bring harm to him and his business. He told me it was his legacy, and I know he and his brothers have worked so hard on growing White Knight Advertising into something beyond what their dad left behind.

"Ready?" Derek asks.

I glare at him, and he just winks at me, pulling the cloth out of my mouth.

"Don't listen to them, Cooper, don't give in to their demands—"

I'm cut off by a blow to the side of my head that sends me toppling to the ground. My head smacks against the cold floor so hard I see a flash of white and then taste blood in my mouth. Derek pulls me up again, by my hair this time and gets up in my face, trying to look intimidating. He doesn't need to try very hard. I won't go down without a fight, though. I spit on him, blood and saliva spraying his chapped lips and greasy, pock-marked face.

His eyes go dark and then he grips my neck, squeezing hard.

"Want to try that again, Sienna?"

"Fuck you," I wheeze, struggling to pull in air.

His hand tightens around my neck as he turns to face the phone, which has been recording everything.

"Five hundred million dollars, Cooper Knight. Wired to the account number attached in the email. If we don't hear from you by tomorrow morning..."

I feel his thumb dig into my windpipe and then everything goes black.

Chapter 13

Cooper

As soon as I walk into the penthouse, I know something is wrong. Sienna isn't here. I hadn't heard from her during the afternoon, but I assumed she just got caught up in another custom order.

Now that I'm here though, I can tell I was wrong. It's hard to explain, but I feel the loss of her. The whole energy of the place is off. It's not just that she's gone – though that is plenty concerning on its own, it's this feeling I can't shake. She's in trouble and I know it.

My blood turns to ice in my veins and my heart thuds heavily in my chest, stealing the air right out of my lungs. I thought it was painful to be without her for those first few days during the fallout of the article being released, but this excruciating ache in my heart at the thought of her being in danger is a thousand times worse.

I barely make it to the couch in time before my legs give out, unable to carry the weight of my body any longer. I put my head between my legs in an attempt to control my breathing. Fuck, the adrenaline is spiking my heartrate making me lightheaded but also ready to pounce and kill a motherfucker.

"Get your shit together, you need to find her," I tell myself.

Taking a deep breath, I call Declan, needing someone here to talk some sense into me and help me come up with a plan.

Ten minutes later, Declan walks into my living room. Okay, more like storms in. He seems to breathe a sigh of relief when he sees me.

"Fuck, Cooper, I couldn't understand half of what you said over the phone, I had no idea if you were dying or what," he growls.

I don't have it in me to apologize, because it feels like I'm dying, not knowing where my kitten is. "It's Sienna. She's gone," I grit out, the words digging into my already broken heart, making me wince.

"She left you?"

"No, she was taken. I'm sure of it."

"Her mom?"

I nod in confirmation. "I have no proof, but I feel it. She's in danger. She's not answering her phone and hasn't contacted me for hours. I have no fucking clue where to even start looking for her. I'm really fucking messed up right now, please just…I don't even fucking know."

"Okay, alright, brother, take a breath. You're no use to her if you pass the fuck out from hyperventilating."

I glare at him but try taking in more deep breaths.

"Hey," Declan says more softly. "I get it. When Luna disappeared on me, I lost my fucking mind. We'll find Sienna, okay?"

"Yeah, yeah," I nod, trying to believe him.

"Let's think of places her mom could be keeping her. The bakery, maybe? It's empty right now, right? Maybe check hotels nearby too. We can contact the airport; in case they fly out."

"That's good. Yeah. I'll go to the bakery. You check out hotels." I launch myself off the couch, energized now that I have a plan.

"Hold up. You shouldn't go alone. What if that Derek guy is as much of a loose cannon as Sienna said he is? What if they have a gun? You need backup. And someone should stay here in case she comes back home."

If I weren't still on the verge of a panic attack, I'd take time to appreciate the fact that he referred to my place as her home. As it is, I need to get the fuck out of here and *do* something to get my sweetness back in my arms where she belongs.

"So what are you suggesting?"

"I think we need to call Ash and have him stay here and make calls to airports and hotels. You know he has some connections that might get him more information than we could get on our own."

"Do you think he'd do that for me?"

"Fuck yeah. He might be jaded and cold, but he's your brother. We'll convince him."

I reluctantly agree and get out my phone. Declan grabs it from me, earning him a growl.

"You're a mess right now," Declan says. "Asher is not going to respond to that. Let me talk to him."

"Hurry up," I grunt.

"Why don't you go change out of your suit and get into something more appropriate for kicking ass while I handle this phone call. You know I don't do well with micromanagement."

I grunt my agreement and change my clothes as quickly as possible. I force air into my lungs before I go back out to the living room with Declan. He's right, I need to calm down so I can think clearly enough to find Sienna. "Hang on, kitten. I'm coming," I whisper into the universe, hoping she somehow hears it, feels it, wherever she is.

"Well?" I say to Declan, a little more forcefully than I mean to. I can't help it. Every minute we stay here is another minute Sienna is unsafe, unprotected.

"Asher is on his way. He'll be here in ten minutes."

"Ten? He lives at least twenty minutes away."

Declan shrugs. "I told him it was urgent and that a life was at stake."

"Thanks," I say, utterly surprised that not only did Asher agree to help out, but he seems to realize the importance of this situation.

I'm pacing back and forth by the time Ash shows up. My muscles are tense, my fists clenching and unclenching at my sides. Asher eyes me up and down, and if I didn't know any better, I'd swear I saw a flicker of concern in his eyes. I know I'm his least favorite brother, seeing as I have a sense of humor and never took dad too seriously. I don't think he hates me, by any means. In fact, sometimes I think he's a little jealous that I have the ability to detach from the job, that I'm not wholly identified by following dad's footsteps.

"What do you need from me?" He asks in the same, cool tone he uses with everyone. His eyes betray his voice, however. I can tell he cares. Why else would he show up?

"Stay here in case Sienna shows up. Call the airport, find out if there's a flight booked for—"

Before I get a chance to finish that sentence, my phone beeps with an email notification. My first instinct is to ignore it. Obviously, I have more important things going on than whatever is happening with work. But it's almost seven at night, which is a weird time to be getting work emails. Something compels me to check it.

"Seriously? I thought this was an emergency," Asher says, clearly not enthused with my decision.

He changes his tone when he sees me start to shake, the color draining from my face. The subject line is simply, *Save Sienna.*

"What is it?" Asher asks at the same time as Declan.

I'm unable to form words, but I motion for them to look at my phone with me as I open the email with trembling hands. There's a video attachment that immediately makes my stomach sour. I don't even read the contents of the email, I just click on the video, fearing the worst.

What I see will forever be burned into my brain. Sienna bound and gagged while some woman in a mask, I'm assuming her mom, strikes her on the face. I tighten my grip on my phone and grit my teeth. Declan pries the phone out of my hand before I crush it. He holds it out so we can all see the rest of the video.

I watch in abject horror as my worst nightmare plays out on the tiny phone screen. Sienna rolls on her back and I see her arm twist at an unnatural angle. Her muffled scream almost does me in, but I have to see the rest of it.

A surge of pride mixes with the fear and adrenaline when I see her fight back. She tries kicking her mother. Her fight doesn't last long, though. Her mom crunches a heel down on Sienna's foot. From the restrained scream and tears flooding her eyes, I can tell the bitch probably broke something.

"Jesus Christ," Asher grunts. I'd agree, but I can't say anything. I can't even breathe.

My kitten shows her claws once again, headbutting her mom right in the face. Sienna is so fucking strong, fighting through her injuries.

"Thatta girl," Declan mumbles. Despite the circumstances, my lip twitches upwards at his comment.

Her mom steps out of the frame, and then a large man, I'm assuming Derek, manhandles her and grumbles some threat in her ear. When he releases her, the duct tape is off of her lips, revealing red marks on her beautiful face where the tape was savagely ripped away.

My kitten looks right at the camera, and fuck, she doesn't look scared or in pain. She looks fierce and determined.

"Don't listen to them, Cooper, don't give in to their demands—"

Derek smacks her so hard she falls over. I snarl and squeeze my fists tightly, so I can feel my nails biting the skin. I don't know how much more of this I can take. I'm going to kill him. I know it. He's living on borrowed time.

He pulls her up by her hair and grips her throat before looking into the camera. "Five hundred million dollars, Cooper Knight. Wired to the account number attached in the email. If we don't hear from you by tomorrow morning..."

I watch as Sienna's face grows red and then purple as his fingers tighten around her neck. She goes limp and he tosses her to the ground. The screen goes black.

My thoughts are all over the fucking place, so much so I can't even form words. I want to tear this whole goddamn city apart until I find her. Then I'm locking her away with me and never letting her out of my sight again.

"Cooper," Asher's voice pierces through my thoughts. His tone is firm, but it's the underlying compassion that pulls me back from the edge.

I look at him and see a fierceness in his eyes, but for once it's not directed at me for being an annoying little shit. I see loyalty and a protective streak a mile wide in his gaze as it bores down on me. That mask of cold indifference he always wears slips a bit, letting me see a glimpse of his humanity.

There's hope for you yet, Ash.

"I know where she is," Asher says. His words are too shocking to believe at first. "It's one of the properties I looked at a while ago when we were considering expanding the New York branch into Brooklyn. The neighborhood was slated to have extensive upgrades, and the property was a good price, but the building was gutted and needed far more work than it was worth. The funding project for the neighborhood got cut shortly after..."

I glare at him, making it perfectly clear I don't give a fuck how he knows about the building. "Let's go there right fucking now!" I growl, storming towards the elevator once again.

Ash grabs my arm, halting my progress. "Be smart about this. We can't just barge in there and crack skulls. They're not going to kill her if they think they're getting money from you. She's their only leverage."

"Typical Asher, always thinking about the bottom line. Sienna is a fucking warrior, but she's broken and bleeding and terrified and I refuse to leave her like for another second," I growl.

"Dammit, Cooper!" Ash yells. "I'm trying to help. All I'm saying is if you storm in there all amped up and without a game plan, you could very well be killed, thus ensuring more harm will come to Sienna."

"Plus, don't you want them to pay for what they've done?" Declan adds. "We have to get the cops involved."

"It'll take too long. I could be halfway there by now, just shut up and let me go!"

Asher and Declan exchange a look. "We're going with you," Asher says in an authoritative voice. "Declan will call the police and tell them the situation. We'll probably get there before them, but they will be there soon enough and they can deal with those degenerates while you get your girl."

"You'd really do that for me?" I ask. I expect something like this from Declan, but not Ash. He nods once and then turns on his heel and heads towards the elevator.

Asher drives us in my Lambo to a neighborhood in Brooklyn that looks like it was in the process of being gentrified before funds ran out. I suppose I heard him say something to that effect earlier, but I wasn't super paying attention.

Declan calls the police and tips them off to the location and the situation. Ash pulls the car into the parking lot of a new apartment building and I give him an odd look. Surely this can't be the same place as the video.

"Don't want to tip them off. Your car is a bit...flashy," Asher explains. At any other time, I'd think his comment on my car was funny. He's always hated it and tells me all the time what a waste of money it is.

We get out and Asher leads the way down one block off the main road and across the street. I can't tell from the outside if it's the same place from the video, but it looks just as rundown and tetanus-ridden, so there's that.

"I think they have her in the basement," Asher whispers as we walk quietly along the back wall of the abandoned building. "I recognized the pipes. They are a hideous orange color and I cannot imagine why anyone—" He stops talking when Declan nudges him, reminding him once again that no one gives a fuck right now how he knew about the building.

We turn the corner and see a rusted metal door propped open by a rotting chunk of plywood.

Declan bends down and pics up a large rock. I quirk an eyebrow up at him until I realize he means to use it as a weapon. I search around the junkyard surrounding the building and pick up a discarded crowbar.

Ash follows suit, finding what appears to be a long extension cord. I give him a look and he shrugs.

"I'd rather restrain the mom instead of knocking her out with my fists, even if she is a monster. I don't know about you, but I don't feel right hitting a woman, ever," he explains.

I nod in understanding, glad that someone is thinking through things enough to make some sort of sense.

We approach the door, which looks like it was pried open crudely with the very same crowbar I have in my hands. We enter the building silently, though I'm positive my brothers can hear my heart cracking my ribs open with how hard it's pounding.

It all happens so fast.

One minute we're descending the stairs into a dimly lit basement, and the next minute all hell breaks loose. There's a hand around my neck, one that could only belong to Derek. I'm slammed against the wall, but I'm able to take a swing with the crowbar. It hits him in the kneecap and he crumples to the floor, crying like the weak-ass motherfucker he is. I stomp kick him in the face for good measure, breaking his nose and knocking him out.

I hear a shrill scream pierce the air and snap my head to the side to see Ash and Declan wrestling with Sienna's mom. She claws Declan, but he pulls her wrist away and wrenches it behind her back while Ash ties her up.

I drop the crowbar with a loud clang and run farther into the dank basement in search of Sienna. When I see her slumped on the floor in the corner of the room, I run to her and drop to my knees. I see her chest moving up and down, so I know she's alive. Thank fuck.

My eyes roam over her tiny body, taking in the damage. I want to wrap her up in my arms and squeeze her tightly into my chest, but I know she's in a lot of pain and I don't want to hurt her more.

Reaching out, I gently brush her dark hair away from her delicate face. She's covered in bruises, the side of her head has a large cut, and her bottom lip is swollen and bloody. Rage boils up inside of me and I am torn between staying here with my kitten and returning to Derek and ending him for good. Ultimately, my desire to be near Sienna wins out.

I search around for something sharp to cut the zip tie from around her wrists. For the first time in my life, I regret not being that guy who carries around a pocketknife. I find a piece of glass and carefully wedge it between Sienna's soft skin and the zip tie. In one swift move, the restraint falls away, and I breathe a sigh of relief when I see I didn't cut her in the process.

She looks so uncomfortable lying on her side with her arms still behind her back. Slowly, so slowly, I move her good arm and pull her into my lap. I resist the urge to hug her close, settling for at least being able to touch her.

Sienna mumbles something and then her eyes flutter open. God, those eyes of hers. Despite everything going on around us, I can't help but get completely lost in them. I see disbelief, pain, and overwhelming relief wash over her as her gorgeous eyes fill up with tears. She tries to sit up but winces against the pain in her shoulder. Or maybe her foot. Or maybe her head. Fuck, she's hurting from so many wounds and there's not a damn thing I can do about it right now.

"Don't move, sweetness," I tell her in the most calming voice I can muster considering there's a lump in my throat and I feel my own eyes filling up with tears.

"Cooper?" She whimpers, her voice all scratchy. It sounds like it hurts for her to even talk. "Are you really here?"

"Shhh, baby, you're okay. Don't talk if it hurts. I'm here. I'm not going anywhere. You're okay now, kitten."

"Sir, we've got it from here," a male voice booms from behind me. I was so caught up in having my Sienna with me again, I didn't even notice the police showed up as well as an EMT crew.

I don't want to let her go, but I know she needs medical attention. Reluctantly, I let the man and his partner, a middle-aged woman, take over. The woman crouches down in front of us, not moving her just yet, and asks what hurts. Sienna answers as best she can, and I fill in what I can from what I saw in the video.

"I'm so sorry, honey, this is going to hurt. I need to move you onto the stretcher now so we can carry you upstairs," the woman says.

"No, no, no..." Sienna whimpers. "Cooper..."

"I'm right here, sweetness. Right here." I turn to the lady who has the stretcher ready, the male EMT standing next to her. "Can I lift her? She's already in my arms."

"Go ahead. Sam here will help you," she says, nodding towards her partner.

Sienna winces as silent tears pour down her bruised cheeks. She doesn't make a sound though, trying to be brave. We get her strapped into the stretcher, Sienna's eyes never leaving mine.

"I'm right here, baby," I reassure her as I follow them up the stairs. It takes every fucking thing in me not to rip it from their hands and carry her to safety myself, but I remind myself these two know more than I do about this stuff, and their goal is to make sure she gets the treatment she needs as quickly as possible. I don't want to fuck that up by being a caveman.

I float through the next few hours. It feels like one excruciating thing after another for Sienna. One of the EMT's pops her shoulder back into place, explaining they needed to get the bone back in its socket before the joint swells. Some of the pain subsides once her shoulder is set.

Next is her foot, which thankfully doesn't require surgery. They had to set her bones back in place there too, which was a hundred times more agonizing than her shoulder, even after a few shots to numb the pain. They set her up with a boot to go with the sling she'll be wearing to prevent her from moving her arm too much while her shoulder is healing. The doctors ruled out a brain bleed, but my sweetness has a nasty concussion, which means no heavy-duty pain meds since they thin the blood and could cause bigger issues.

After she's been cleaned up and bandaged, Sienna gives her statement to the police. Shortly after, we get the all-clear to go home. I've been so caught up with being by Sienna's side every second, that I forgot I don't have a car here. I make a quick call to Declan and have him send his driver over. This terrible day needs to end, and the only way I'll be able to fully breathe again is holding Sienna in my arms and watching her sleep.

Chapter 14

Cooper

I carry Sienna inside once we get back to our place. She has crutches and a wheelchair that came with her from the hospital, but the safest place for her is in my arms. I don't set her down until we're in the master bathroom. She got cleaned up a bit while she was in the hospital, but I know she needs to wash off more than just the lingering dirt and blood.

"You okay to sit here, sweetness?" I ask as I place her on the edge of the tub while kneeling down in front of her, keeping her steady with my hands on her waist.

"I'm good," she rasps, coughing a bit. It pains me to hear her struggling with such a simple thing as talking.

I want to kiss her so damn bad, but she's so sore and tired. I don't even know where I could press my lips on her that wouldn't hurt. That's the last thing I want to do. As if reading my thoughts, Sienna cups my cheek and leans in to rest her forehead on mine.

"Sienna..." I whisper, breathing her in. She smells like the sterile hospital, and a bit like blood, but underneath it all, I smell sweetness and spice. My Sienna. My kitten. *Mine.*

We stay like that for a few moments, but I need to get her cleaned up and in bed. I pull myself away from her and place a gentle kiss on her forehead. Keeping her steady with one hand, I reach over and turn the water on, letting it warm up before putting the stopper in.

While the tub fills up a little bit, I carefully remove her boot and sling and take off the scrubs she wore home from the hospital. It hits me again how small she is. Yes, she's badass, she's a fighter, she's a fucking goddess, but in this moment, she's so fragile. Sienna looks up at me with a mix of trust, adoration, and complete exhaustion.

"I'm just gonna give you a sponge bath, okay, kitten?"

"Okay, Cooper," she whispers.

Kneeling in front of her, I dip a washcloth in the water and load it up with soap before gently wipe her face, her neck, her perfect little breasts. I'm filled with anger once again as I see her precious body littered with scrapes and bruises. Taking a deep breath, I let go of every negative emotion. I just need to be here with her, take care of her, and love her.

When I get to Sienna's back, she leans forward, resting her head on my shoulder. I can feel the weight of the day in her muscles, the way she melts into me like she can't hold herself up any longer.

"Almost done, baby," I whisper as I wash her back. I drop the washcloth and opt to use my hands instead. I keep her steady with one hand on her lower back while the other one massages soap into her neck and back.

Sienna sighs, her breath tickling the skin on my neck. I work the knots in her back with a tender touch, careful to avoid her sore shoulder.

"Thank you," Sienna says, her voice so small and broken.

"Always, sweetness. I'll always take care of you."

Sensing the exhausting pulling her under, I rinse off her back and dry her off before carrying her to bed and throwing one of my shirts over her. I prop her foot up on a pillow and get her all set up on my bed, *our* bed. She's asleep almost instantly, soft little snores pouring out of her lips.

I set up shop in the chair beside the bed, content to watch over her as she sleeps. The doctor said I needed to wake her up every few hours to check on her concussion. I have a book next to me on the nightstand, but I don't even look at it. I'm too fixed on watching Sienna breathe and reminding myself that she's really here.

My phone buzzes in my pocket and seeing that it's well after two a.m., I know it has to be one of my brothers. Aside from the brief request to Declan about using his driver, I haven't talked to either one of them. Pulling my phone out of my pocket, I see it's Asher. Not who

I was expecting. I take the call out in the hallway so as not to disturb Sienna.

"Ash, hey," I say quietly.

"How is she?" He asks. Asher is a bit gruff, but it means a lot that he's trying and that he cares enough to follow up with me. Today has definitely been a turning point for us.

"We're home now. She's resting. Fucked up her foot and shoulder pretty bad, she's got a concussion, but all in all, the doctors said she was lucky."

Asher grunts in acknowledgment. There's a pause, neither one of sure how to proceed. Usually, we only talk when Asher is yelling at me about something or giving me a hard time. It's been years since we've just held a conversation, let alone talked about anything so personal.

"And…you?" He asks, sounding about as unsure of our conversation as I am. "How are you doing with…everything?"

I smile at his attempt to be human with me. My first instinct is to tell him I'm just glad to have Sienna back, which is true, but there's so much more to it than that. I decide that if he's willing to call me in the middle of the night and ask how I'm doing, the least I can do is be honest with him.

I sigh heavily, collecting my thoughts. "Ash… Fuck. I'm relieved that she's here with me, but I'm scared something else is going to happen. I'm furious that I couldn't protect her. And honestly, every time I close my eyes, clips from that fucking video play out in my mind. I don't know what she needs from me, you know?"

At this point I'm not so much looking for a response, I just need to talk it out. Who would have thought Asher would be the one to listen?

"I mean, I can nurse her back to health, but what's the best way to protect her?" I continue. "Rationally, I know the threat of her mom and Derek is gone now that they are going away for a long time, but I still feel like I failed her. Now everything feels like a threat to her safety. Do I lock her away in the penthouse? Bring her with me everywhere I go?

But what kind of life is that? Do we move? Will she want to stay in the city?"

There's more silence on the line while my questions linger unanswered.

"You've always been good at this sort of stuff. The nurturing and whatever," Ash says after a few moments. His voice is almost...soft. "Remember when mom was going to have the rose garden torn out because she decided she didn't like roses anymore? You were just nine or ten, but you said you wanted to keep it, that you'd do all the work. Typical mom pretty much forgot all about it the next day, but you were true to your word. You did all this research and made me take you to the store to get gardening supplies even though we had a gardener who said he'd do it all. Those roses were dead, I was sure of it, but you figured out what they needed to flourish. You've always been...I don't know. Aware of things. People. You're good at anticipating needs and following through. That's what makes you so good in your role at the company, too."

I'm stunned into silence. It's the most he's said to me about non-company related things in probably a decade, and definitely the first time he's complimented me. Asher clears his throat and continues.

"I'm just saying. You have good instincts. And Sienna will be easier to take care of than roses because she can talk. All you have to do is listen."

I can tell the moment is too intense for him. Shit, it's almost too intense for me. So, I go for a joke.

"Damn, Ash, who knew you were such a sap?"

"Must be the adrenaline crash," he replies, though we both know that ended hours ago. Which reminds me...

"Thank you for today, Asher. I mean it. I don't know what I would have done without—"

"It's fine. No thanks necessary," he says, snapping back into his cold, detached demeanor. I'll let him have this out.

"You know what this means though, right?"

He sighs in response. "What's that?"

"You're gonna have to get another tux for the wedding. I haven't asked her yet, but I always thought she'd like a winter wedding. That gives you a few months to come up with a best man speech. Maybe even bring a date?"

"Wonderful," he deadpans.

"It really is," I chuckle.

We're quiet for a beat, then Ash clears his throat. "Get some rest, Coop."

"You too, brother."

He hangs up and I stare at my phone with a big grin on my face. Looks like the cold-hearted bastard isn't quite as immune to having feelings as he wants everyone to believe. I've always known it, but it's been years since he's let his mask slip.

I shake my head and walk back into the room, resuming my position on the chair next to Sienna. It's been a little over an hour and a half, but I can't wait another second to check on her. I reach out and stroke her forehead, the only place that isn't bruised. Tucking some hair behind her ear, I lean down and place soft kisses along her hairline. I feel her stir slightly, so I lean back and take in her face, still so beautiful even with her scrapes and bruises.

"Mmm, Cooper?" She whispers as her eyes flutter open.

"I'm here, sweetness. Sorry I had to wake you up, I'm supposed to make sure your pupils aren't dilated, and you can hold a conversation."

"What kind of conversation?"

I grin at that. "I think you just passed the test."

"And I didn't even study," she murmurs, a tired little smile on her lips. Fuck, she's so precious, so pure in this moment. My heart aches just looking at her.

"Go back to sleep now, kitten. I'll be right here."

She mumbles something and then closes her eyes. I sit back in the chair and count her breaths. Sienna's eyes flicker open and she looks right at me.

"Why aren't you in bed with me?" She asks.

"I don't want to risk hurting you accidentally."

"You won't. Aren't you tired?"

"Baby, I'm not sleeping tonight whether I'm in the bed or not."

Confusion spreads across her face. "Why not? It was such an impossible night; I know you're exhausted."

"I can't fuck up with your care, Sienna. I'm supposed to wake you up every few hours. You're too important for me to screw up your safety. Again." She looks like she's going to protest, but I continue. "Besides, I can't sleep. I can hardly close my eyes without picturing you in that basement..."

"Cooper," she says so gently my heart breaks and heals at the same time. "Please come lay next to me? I think it will help us both. We can set an alarm for two hours."

My initial reaction is to stand my ground, but Asher's words come back to me. *All you have to do is listen.*

Sienna is telling me she needs me to be next to her, so of course, I'm going to go lie down next to her.

"Okay, kitten," I tell her before setting the alarm on my phone.

I walk around to the other side of the bed and strip down to my boxer briefs. I slowly crawl into bed, not wanting to shake the mattress or jostle Sienna at all.

"You're still too far away," she says.

"What if I roll over and hurt you? Or accidentally kick your bad foot? Or elbow you in the head?"

"Have you ever kicked me or elbowed me in the head before?" She teases. I'm not in the joking mood, for once in my life.

"Sienna, I'm serious. I already hurt you by failing to protect you. There's no way in hell I'm going to allow myself to hurt you again."

"What do you mean you failed to protect me?" Her brow is furrowed in confusion, but then her eyes go wide with realization. "You think it's your fault my mom found me?"

"I know it is. I put the article out there, and then even when I tried keeping you protected here in the penthouse, I still failed to save you from her. This is all my fault. Every single cut, bruise, broken bone...it's all because of me, Sienna. I'm so fucking sorry, so sorry. I..."

She places her hand on the middle of the bed, clearly trying to reach out to me even though I'm too far away. Tentatively, I scoot closer and gently wrap my hand around hers. Sienna closes her eyes and breathes in deep.

I take time to brush the pad of my thumb over her knuckles and then uncurl her hand, tracing the inside of her palm with my fingers.

"Look at me, Cooper," Sienna says. I have no choice but to follow her command. "My mom is a fucking psychopath, and *she* is the one who hurt me. She hurt me long before I ever moved out here and met you. The article may have set things in motion, but you can't take responsibility for her deranged plans. That's not on you. I don't want you bringing it up again, especially after tonight."

Sienna takes another deep breath before continuing. "You have done everything in your power to keep me safe, and more than that, you've made me feel so cherished. Like I matter. Like you see me and know me and truly, truly want me. I've never had that. So while I'm not a fan of *how* I came to be in your care, the truth is, I'm so grateful that I am. I'm grateful for every day we spend together." She laces our fingers together and tugs me towards her. I inch closer and closer until she lets go of my hand and traces her fingers over my face.

"Sweetness..."

"Let me finish. I'm going for extra credit on my conversation test," she grins at me. I turn my head and kiss her fingertips. "You weren't in the room when I gave my statement to the police, so you don't know how they got to me. Cooper, I wasn't here in the penthouse."

"What?"

"It was so stupid, I know. I got comfortable here with you and the danger felt so far away. I ran some errands, I wanted to surprise you with a few things. Obviously, the kind of surprise you got was *not* the one I intended. So it wasn't your fault at all. And it wasn't mine. Let's place the blame and anger on the ones who deserve it – Derek and my mom."

I'm overwhelmed by her confession. She's forgiving me, but also releasing me from my own prison of guilt. The fact that she's grateful to be in my care, fuck, that she even *admits* to wanting my care...it's everything. To hear her say I make her feel cherished and wanted drains the last of the fear from my heart and replaces it with such love and joy. God, she's so incredible.

"Cooper?" Her sweet voice brings me back from my thoughts.

"Yeah, baby?"

"Are you mad? Did I say too much? What are you thinking about?"

Shit, I must have been lost in my head a lot longer than I thought. Suddenly, I'm overcome with exhaustion. It's like I was holding out until I heard how they were able to get her, and now that it's all out there in the open, I find I'm struggling to even keep my eyes open.

"I'm not mad, sweetness. And you didn't say too much. Fuck, Sienna, all I've ever wanted is to show you how much I love you."

She gasps quietly, and I realize what I said. Of course, I love her. I have pretty much since the first moment I saw her. But I was hoping to tell her in a much more romantic setting.

"You love me," she whispers. It's not a question, it's more like she's testing out the idea in her head.

"More than you could ever know."

She smiles through her tears, those beautiful eyes of hers sparkling for the first time since everything went down. "Then can you come over here and hold me? I just need to feel you."

I scoot closer to her once again and settle down by her side. She's all propped up on pillows, laying on her back. I turn on my side to face her, letting my eyes roam over her features and drink her in. Sienna takes my hand and lays it across her tummy, my palm resting on her hip. Then she places her soft little hand over mine and laces our fingers together.

"I don't want to hurt you," I say again.

"You won't. I trust you."

Her words mean everything to me. Tentatively, I kiss the exposed skin on her good shoulder, the one closest to me. Sienna sighs contentedly, so I press another kiss into her warm skin before resting my head on her shoulder.

"I love you, too, Cooper," Sienna whispers so softly I almost don't hear it.

I prop myself up and look at her, but she's already sound asleep. Nuzzling back down against her body, I finally allow myself to relax and join her in sleep.

Chapter 15

Sienna

The last six weeks have flown by. Cooper officially sold the bakery back to me, although I refused to keep the extra money that the original contract outlined. Instead, Cooper offered to give Mad Batter Bakery a complete marketing makeover, which I agreed to now that the threat of mom and Derek is long gone.

The trial moved quickly as there was video proof of their torture and blackmail as well as the eyewitness accounts from Cooper, Declan, Asher, and me. Thanks to the cutthroat lawyers Cooper has on retainer, mom and Derek will be serving several life sentences. I don't feel sorry for them in the least.

I originally stayed with Cooper so he could take care of me during my recovery, but he asked me to move in officially about a week after everything went down. He said he wouldn't sleep knowing I wasn't by his side. I couldn't argue with that, because I knew I'd be the same way. Plus, Mandy, my loyal bakery assistant, needed a place to live, so I happily let her have the apartment above the bakery.

There's one more big life change that I just found out about this morning. I thought about the best way to tell Cooper all morning and finally came up with what I think is a brilliant plan.

I just got back from grocery shopping and a second trip to the little French boutique I visited right before I was taken. I thought I'd have a flashback or something while walking by the alley where Derek grabbed me, but I only felt safe and confident. Part of it was knowing Derek will live the rest of his life in a prison cell, but the bigger part was because I knew Cooper would always protect me and always come after me if anything ever happened.

The lady remembered me from my original visit and gave me a knowing look when I went for the same pieces again. I'm sure she assumed my lover, as she so delicately put it, ripped up my pretty lingerie in a fit of passion. She doesn't have to know what really happened. Plus, I hope to be coming back here again soon to buy more pieces for Cooper to destroy.

We haven't had sex since before I was taken. It wasn't possible for me for the first few weeks – I really did take a beating and it took a while for me to recover. After about three weeks, all my bruises were healed, my shoulder was back to normal, and the only thing reminding me of that awful night was the boot on my foot. I got that off last week, but Cooper still treats me with kid gloves when it comes to sex. He thinks me having an orgasm would still be too strenuous on my body, so yeah. I haven't cum in six whole weeks.

That was never a problem before I met Cooper, but he got me all addicted to him and the things he does to my body, and then he made me quit cold turkey. My only solace is that he also hasn't had an orgasm this whole time, so at least I know he's suffering too. It also gives me hope that my plan to seduce him will work, especially after officially getting a clean bill of health from my doctor this morning at my very last, post-boot removal check-up.

Cooper really wanted to go with me, but I knew he had a big meeting today and I promised him I'd FaceTime him before and after. He wanted to be on the phone the whole time *during* the appointment, but I'm glad I talked him out of that.

"What smells so good, sweetness?" Cooper calls out from the hallway.

I check the clock on the oven and see he's about thirty minutes earlier than I thought. No worries. My plan is still perfect.

"Probably the dinner I'm cooking for my man," I reply with a smile as Cooper walks into the kitchen.

I'm still not used to how freaking handsome he is, especially in his expensive, tailor-made suit. And no, it's not just my lack of sex lately that's saying that. He really is that freaking sexy. That dark hair coupled with his bright blue eyes, easy smile, and dimples, Cooper really is just too gorgeous for words. Let's not even get started on his incredible muscles and gigantic…

"You okay, baby?" Cooper asks, making his way over to me and wrapping me up in his arms. We might not have had sex in weeks, but he's always given me plenty of hugs and sweet touches, knowing that I crave that from him after being alone for so long. And also because it's Cooper and I just crave *him* all the time.

"Mmhmm, just thinking about what you're hiding under that sexy suit," I murmur before kissing the side of his neck.

Cooper's breath catches in his throat and I feel his muscles involuntarily flex against me, his cock twitching as well. I grin into his tender flesh and then nip at him ever so slightly. I feel him harden even more against me. This is going to be easier than I thought.

"Fuck, you can't say shit like that, Sienna. I want you so damn bad."

"So take me," I practically purr, staring him straight in the eyes.

I watch his pupils dilate and his nostrils flare. I go for the kill and bite my bottom lip. That does it.

Cooper tugs the hair at the back of my neck and takes my mouth in a hungry kiss. We've kissed since everything happened, of course. Well, once my bruises started to fade. It was the longest week of my life. But all of our kisses have been sweet. Tender. Careful.

There is nothing sweet about this kiss.

It's filthy and forceful and so perfect. I push him back so he's pinned between me and the counter. No escaping now. Pressing my body closer to his, I rub up and down, giving us both the friction we need.

Cooper groans into the kiss, the first sign of actual primal desire he's shown in weeks. His hands roam down my back, squeezing my hips and then landing on my ass where he holds me in place while he grinds into me.

My fingers trail down his defined chest, feeling him up through his nice dress shirt that I want to rip off of him. All in good time. The spell is broken, however, when my hand drifts down and palms his cock.

Cooper hisses and pulls away from me slightly, pressing his lips to my forehead and breathing in deeply.

"Shit," he mumbles into my skin. I giggle and roll my hips into him one last time, making him growl softly. "Kitten..." he groans, sounding in pain. "Don't tease me."

I push off of him and turn towards the oven, swinging my hips as I walk away from him. Looking over my shoulder, I see a breathless Cooper holding onto the counter for support. It makes me feel sexy and powerful and confident in my plan. "I'll be good," I say. "For now."

Cooper clears his throat and wipes a hand down his face, trying to gain his composure. "So," he finally says. "What's for dinner?"

"Creamy pesto chicken and potatoes. I also have a dessert I think you're going to love," I tell him while stirring the sauce that's been simmering on the stovetop.

"Oh yeah?" He says, his voice lower and much closer than I thought it would be.

Cooper is right behind me, his breath tickling the back of my neck while his hands skim over my hips before grabbing them and pulling me back so my ass is pressed against his erection. It's even larger now.

"I thought we were being good," I whisper.

"So good," he replies in between peppering kisses down the side of my neck. Cooper's large hands move from my hips down my thighs, lifting up the skirt of my dress to trace feather-light circles on the exposed skin of my thighs.

"So good," I moan in agreement. His fingers tease me, moving so slowly up the insides of my thighs, closer, closer, closer.

I spin around in his arms before he reaches my center and discovers my lacy lingerie, looping my arms around his neck and biting his bottom lip. Cooper takes the hint and shoves his tongue into my mouth, devouring me all over again with hungry strokes of his tongue.

"Jesus," he grunts once we break apart.

The timer for the chicken goes off, and I grin up at him, giving him one more chaste kiss on his lips before turning back towards the food I've prepared. "Hungry for dinner?" I ask.

"I'm hungry for something, alright," he mumbles.

I laugh and place the pan of chicken and potatoes on the stovetop to cool a bit before serving.

We manage to get through dinner without too much groping and making out. Cooper tries to clear the table, but I swat his hands away and tell him to stay put while I get the dessert.

I'd be lying if I said I wasn't a little nervous about this part. I'm pretty confident he'll love this surprise, but it's kind of a game-changer and any girl would be nervous in my position. Taking a deep breath, I arrange the special dessert on a serving tray. Lemon cupcakes with raspberry filling and vanilla bean frosting. Each cupcake has a different design on top – a baby bottle, a diaper, little booties, a rattle, and so on.

I set the tray in front of Cooper and stand back, waiting for his reaction.

"These are cute," he says. "Are they left over from a baby shower custom order?" He asks, eyeing each cupcake.

"No..." I reply.

"A kid's birthday?"

"Nope."

I see the moment it dawns on him. His eyes grow wide with disbelief as he lifts is head and looks right at me. His gaze drops to my hands, covering my non-existent baby bump.

"Are you saying...?"

I nod my head and smile anxiously. His look isn't giving away anything other than shock.

Cooper is out of his chair and down on his knees in front of me in a flash, placing tender kisses all over my belly. I laugh as I choke back tears.

"I love you so much, little one," he says into my stomach in between kisses. "I'm going to protect you always and fill your life with so much love," he promises.

I rake my fingers through his hair, causing him to look up at me. There are tears in his eyes and a huge grin on his face.

"You're pregnant," he says, making me laugh again.

"So I've been told," I nod.

Cooper stands up and wraps his strong arms around me, lifting me up and twirling me around. I laugh kiss him all over his face. Finally, we stop spinning, and Cooper slides me down his body until my feet hit the ground. He cradles my head in his hands and looks at me with so much love I feel like I might start crying. When Cooper's thumbs wipe away my tears, I realize I've done just that.

"Sienna, my kitten, god I love you so much," he says softly before kissing me. One kiss rolls into another and another until we're both panting for air. Cooper keeps me close to him, pressing my body into his while we both catch our breath.

He leads me over to the couch and sits down, pulling me into his lap. "When did you find out?" He asks, one hand pressed to my belly possessively while the other rubs circles on my back.

"This morning at my doctor's appointment. They did bloodwork the first time I was brought into the hospital, of course, but I guess it was too soon to tell. Since today was my last scheduled appointment, they did a full workup again and the doctor called me a few hours later to let me know."

"How are you feeling? Do you need anything? Vitamins, right? And maternity clothes? Shit, I don't know how to put on a diaper. Which room do you want to be the nursery? Should we move out of the city since we're starting a family? What if—"

I cut him off with a kiss, hoping to stop him from spiraling out of control. Cooper is already so protective of me, and I know being pregnant is going to make him crazy with the need to take care of me. Of *us*.

"There's more," I whisper into his lips once I've kissed him into submission.

"More?" He croaks out, an adorably worried look on his face.

"Mmhmm," I hum before readjusting myself on his lap so I'm straddling him. Cooper's hands automatically find my ass and squeeze, causing my hips to roll forward. "The doctor said I can have all the filthy, mind-blowing, toe-curling sex I want," I purr, looking him in the eye as I slowly lift my dress over my head, revealing my red, barely-there lingerie set. "He said it was perfectly safe for me to cum long and hard, again, and again, and—"

Cooper spanks me, causing me to gasp and buck my hips. He groans and squeezes my ass, thrusting up as I grind down on him. "Are you telling me you talked to your doctor about orgasms?" He growls into the side of my neck before sucking and biting the tender flesh there.

My body is buzzing, vibrating with a need so great I'm almost afraid of the release it will bring. I can't form any more words; my body is completely given over to lust and longing. I simply moan in reply, hoping he can sense how desperate I am to cum.

"Looks like I'm going to have to remind you what it means to be mine, kitten," Cooper says as he continues trailing kisses down my neck and shoulder. "Fuck, you're so fucking sexy in this," he growls before pulling the cup of my bra down with his teeth.

One minute we're making out on the couch and the next minute I'm in his arms as he carries me down the hall to our room. Cooper kisses and bites and loves every inch of me before stripping me down and getting naked himself. He has me spread out for him on the bed while he stands before me, stroking his cock.

"Goddamn, sweetness," he grits out, squeezing the tip of his cock and closing his eyes. Cooper takes a deep breath and then opens his eyes, staring right at me with dirty intentions. I bite my lip and spread my legs open, showing him what he's been missing.

"I need you, Cooper," I tell him breathlessly.

He kneels down in between my legs and nuzzles my belly, placing sweet kisses right where your baby is growing. I can't help the watery smile that thought brings to my face. Cooper looks up with the same expression. I feel closer to him than I ever have.

Cooper continues trailing kisses up from my belly, over my ribs, in between my breasts, up my neck, my jaw, and then he hovers over my mouth.

"Are you sure you're ready for me, kitten? Once I get inside of you, I don't know if I'll be able to control myself. It's been too damn long."

"And whose fault is that?" I tease.

Cooper nips my bottom lip, pulling it through his teeth and then licking away the sting. "I'm serious, Sienna. I need to hear you say the words."

I cup his face in my hands and stare into his breath-taking blue eyes. The same blue eyes that captivated me all those weeks ago when I stumbled into his arms. The same blue eyes that pleaded with me to give him a second chance. The same blue eyes that knocked down all of my walls and quickly became my new home. The same blue eyes I hope to gaze into for the rest of my life.

"I need you, Cooper," I tell him again, though my tone is different this time. I *do* need him, and not just to give me an orgasm, but to feel the closeness that can only come from being connected to him from the inside out.

"I need you too, Sienna," he whispers before kissing me.

He sits back on his heels and runs his hands all over my body, mapping me out and making me quiver in anticipation. He starts by gliding his fingers down my shoulders, then over my breasts, stopping briefly to tweak my nipples. Lower, lower, lower his hands roam, until they grasp my thighs and spread me wide open.

Cooper dips two fingers into my slit, groaning when he feels how wet I am. He rubs my clit and plunges two fingers into my pulsing, wet hole while I writhe beneath him. Cooper withdraws his fingers and wipes my honey over my lips before kissing it off. I swear I almost cum from that alone.

I wiggle my hips, trying to get him where I need him most. Cooper takes the hint and reaches down, positioning his cock at my entrance. He surges forward, hitting the end of me in one, long thrust.

"Fuck, Sienna, god I missed you so much," he groans, holding himself still inside of me so I can get used to the feeling again.

I whimper and nod my head in agreement. Cooper claims my mouth again, sucking on my tongue while pulling out and setting a frantic pace. It feels so fucking good to have him inside of me again, his fat cock stretching me and filling me over and over.

My legs tighten around his hips and my hands grip the tight muscles in his back. I hang on to this powerful beast as he fucks me with rough strokes, imprinting himself on me, in me for all of time. No one will ever make me feel this way. No one but my Cooper. My love.

I feel his mouth on my neck and his thumb circling my clit. Gasping for air, my spine arches, lifting me off the bed as I dig my nails into his back. My orgasm is right there, so close, my muscles stretch as my body reaches out for it...

Cooper pinches my clit and I explode, crying out his name as my pussy spasms around him, trying to suck him in deeper.

"Jesus, you feel incredible, coming around my cock like a good girl. Let's see if I can get you to do it again."

With that, Cooper stands up and pulls me with him, tugging me towards the nearest wall. My pussy clenches just thinking about what he has in mind. He spins me around so I'm facing the wall, my back to his front. I feel his hands skimming up and down my body, stroking my skin and keeping me right on edge.

"Hands on the wall, sweetness," he whispers into my neck before biting the skin there and licking away the sting. I do as he says, and am rewarded with his fingers in my pussy, circling my clit and making me leak my juices all over his hand. "I'm going to make you cum so hard, kitten, so fucking hard. Goddamn, I want to tear you apart and feast on you and fuck you. You make me crazy with need, baby girl."

I moan at his words, rubbing my ass against him over and over. Cooper snarls, biting me again. It hurts so good and I love knowing he feels this need to mark me. He kisses the skin so tenderly and runs his nose up and down the same spot.

"After you're so thoroughly fucked you can't even move, I'm going to kiss it all better, I promise. I'll always take care of you. Always, Sienna."

This is my Cooper. Sexy as fuck, dominating, rough, and wild. But somehow also gentle, sweet, and caring. He's perfect and all mine. Forever.

Slowly his cock sinks inside of me. I feel pain and pleasure; ecstasy and agony. He stretches me out with his thick dick, sliding it along my walls as he pushes forward ever so much. There's so much tension wrapped up in my muscles, I feel like I might just burst. When he thrusts all the way up inside of me, I do just that. I cum unexpectedly around his cock, my pussy snapping around him and pulling him deeper inside of me.

"Fuck, sweetness. I'm not done with you yet," he rasps in my ear before biting my neck and kissing away the sting.

Cooper grips my hips tightly and pounds into me, fucking me through my orgasm. My body shakes with each powerful stroke, his balls slapping my clit making my mind short circuit with a mix of white-hot bliss that borders on pain.

My arms give out and Cooper presses me into the wall with his hard, hot body. Another orgasm blooms inside of me, but I can't quite reach it. I'm on a razor's edge, the sharp pain and intense pleasure making me sob with need.

Without warning, Cooper pulls out and spins me around. He has me in his arms, my legs wrapped around his hips and my back against the wall before the fog has cleared my mind. Cooper slams into me, digging his fingertips into my ass where he's holding me up.

"Ohmygod, Cooper, yes..." I whimper as he fucks me savagely against the wall.

"That's it, kitten, cum for me again, I need to feel this cunt squeeze my big cock," he grunts.

Cooper takes my mouth in a hungry, desperate kiss, biting and sucking and drinking me down while his dick splits me open again and again. I tear my mouth away from his, gasping for air as my muscles tense to the point of pain.

I feel my orgasm growing, each thrust winding me up tighter and tighter, again and again, higher and higher, until it all comes crashing down around me. I bury my face in Cooper's neck and scream my release as I cling to him.

"You're perfect, so damn beautiful," he whispers as I fall apart in his arms.

Cooper peels me off the wall, still holding me in his arms. He sits on the edge of the bed, with me straddling him, his dick still rock fucking hard inside of me. I don't know how he's keeping it together. I've already lost track of how many orgasms I've had.

"Ready for more, kitten?"

I nod and sink my teeth into the firm flesh of his shoulder, earning me the sexy growl of a man barely able to control himself. Good. I don't want him to. "Fuck me, Cooper," I moan into his ear before pulling his earlobe in between my teeth.

That's all the permission he needs.

Cooper grabs my ass with both hands, spreads it wide, and thrusts into me, fucking me so deep, so rough. I throw my head back and gasp as he fucks the air right out of my lungs, the scream out of my throat, my soul out of my body.

I bounce up and down on his cock, my pussy raw and sore and so sensitive, but ready to take another beating. Cooper looks between us where we're joined, and groans, almost sound like he's in pain.

"Fucking Christ, sweetness. Love watching you take all of me like a good girl. This pussy is mine, fucking *mine*." He tilts my hips slightly and hammers up into my g-spot, the intense pleasure wracking my body with every stroke.

It hits me like lightning. The orgasm starts in my spine and then shoots down to my pussy, wet and throbbing between my legs. I cum all over his fat cock, unable to stop as he spreads me wider and fucks me harder. I take all of him and cum again, letting it spread all over his cock as he growls his pleasure, biting my lips and spanking my ass, tearing me in two with each thrust.

"Oh god," I gasp, pushing down on his length and holding myself there. My legs quiver and I feel weak. I whimper in his arms.

It's not possible for me to cum again. I'm sure another orgasm would give me a heart attack. And yet...something is happening. A pressure so intense, so all-consuming I can't breathe. I'm a little scared my body can't take it, but as always, Cooper seems to know me better than I know myself.

"I've got you, Sienna. Let go for me, baby, let it happen."

"Cooper...I can't...I don't..."

"Cum for me, love, cum for me again."

Cooper slams into me one last time, breaking me wide open and releasing the ball of pressure built up deep inside of me. I gush for him as I cum violently. Something is pressing down on my bladder, but I don't have time to worry about it. My pussy just keeps knotting around Cooper's cock, again and again, leaking more juices between us and making a mess of the sheets.

"Jesus, you're squirting all over me, baby, fuck, fuck, fuck..." Cooper roars his release, sloppy sounds mixed with cries of passion filling the room as we cum together over and over.

I go limp in his arms, my body numb and devoid of strength. Cooper holds me tightly and thrusts into me once, twice, three times, before collapsing backward on the bed.

When I open my eyes again, Cooper and I are lying in bed on our sides, facing each other. Cooper is holding me close and tracing a line from my shoulder down to my hip and back again.

"Hey," he says softly, those blue eyes of his sparkling with such adoration my heart stops in my chest.

"Hi," I whisper.

"You okay? That was..."

"Intense."

Cooper nods, worry flashing across his features. "Did I hurt you?"

I shake my head no and scoot up to kiss him on the lips. "I'm so good, Cooper. I missed all of this. More than I thought possible. Tonight was perfect."

Relief washes over him as he smiles so sweetly at me. "*You're* perfect, kitten. So beautiful and precious to me."

I smile and reach out to run my fingers through his hair but stop when I see something sparkly on my hand.

"Cooper..."

"Yes, love?" He grins.

"I'm wearing a ring," I say stupidly because, holy shit, it's *huge* and gorgeous and not at all how I thought this night would end. It's a million times better.

"Hmm, what are you going to do about it?"

Once I finally pull my eyes away from the princess cut diamond glittering on my finger, I see Cooper giving me his most devastating smile, one with a hint of mischief and a whole lotta love.

"I guess I should probably keep it," I shrug nonchalantly.

"You better," he growls, rolling on top of me and pinning me down with his body.

I smile up at him and bite my lip, loving the tender fierceness of his gaze. I don't even know how that's possible, but there's no other way to describe the look he's giving me right now. Something dawns on me and I have to ask.

"How long have you had this? You're not just marrying me cuz I'm knocked up, you already had this before I told you."

Cooper looks taken aback at first, but quickly recovers, giving me a chaste kiss and then resting his forehead on mine.

"Of course, I'm not marrying you because you're having my baby. I love you, Sienna. I have ever since you slapped me and shocked the hell out of me in the best way possible. I bought that ring the day I brought you back to the penthouse after you got that package from your mom. It was always my intention to marry you, I've just been waiting for the perfect moment to ask."

Tears well up in my eyes, but I blink them away. "Technically, you didn't ask, you know," I tease, though I'm barely keeping it together.

Cooper kisses me deeply, one long, drugging kiss leading to another. He flips our positions so I'm on top of him. One hand slides to the back of my neck and guides me so I'm resting my forehead on his.

"Sweetness, will you be my best friend, my lover, my wife? Will you let me love you and take care of you and our growing family? Will you laugh with me and fight with me and challenge me to be a better man every day for the rest of our lives?"

I'm full-on crying now, there's just really no stopping it. "Yes," I whisper. "I want that with you."

Cooper closes the distance between us and kisses me with such an overwhelming vulnerability I can taste his promises and love. I give all of it right back to him. I finally feel complete, safe, grounded.

"Love you so much, kitten. So goddamn much," he whispers into my skin as he presses his lips to my forehead.

Cooper tucks me into his chest and begins rubbing my back in calming circles.

"Love you more," I whisper, turning my head to place a kiss over his heart.

He chuckles and hugs me closer. "We'll see about that, sweetness. I can't wait to prove you wrong."

Epilogue

Cooper

"Why are we even having a baby shower? You're a billionaire, it's not like we need people buying us baby shit," Sienna whines from her little nest on the couch.

I smile and walk over to her, dropping a kiss on top of her head. "*We're* billionaires, sweetness. What's mine is yours, you know that."

She glares at me. "That's *so* not the point."

I grin and hand her the bowl of ice cream she asked for. "The baby shower is to celebrate. People are happy for us and I want to show off my little family."

"You mean you want to show off your elephant of a fiancé?" She grumbles.

"Hey now, none of that." I sit down next to her and reach for her ice cream in an attempt to get her to look at me. That was a mistake. She growls at me, which makes me simultaneously shudder in fear and also grow painfully hard in my jeans. My pregnant fiancé is sexy as fuck, even more so when she's grumpy and needs me to remind her how beautiful she is.

"Cooper, I'm gigantic. And I have another ten weeks to go."

"You're gorgeous, and you're carrying my babies. There's nothing on this whole fucking Earth that turns me on like knowing I can hold my entire family in my arms like this," I tell her truthfully as I wrap her up in my embrace.

We found out a few weeks after I proposed that Sienna is having twins, and I could not be more thrilled. I know she's excited too. The twins already have a closet full of clothes we've been told they'll grow out of in a month, but I don't give a fuck. She gets so giddy, and then weepy when she sees those little outfits and shoes, so of course, we have to buy every single one. What's the point of having all of this money if we can't spend it on our kids?

Sienna sighs in my arms and snuggles deeper. "You always know just what to say to bring your hormonal baby momma back from a full-on melt-down."

I grin and kiss the tip of her nose. "You have a right to feel whatever you want to feel, love. This is supposed to be a good thing, a *fun* thing, but I can cancel it if you really don't want to have a baby shower."

"No, no, I want this," she says a little more determined. "Plus, I'd be letting Luna down too, and only a heartless bastard would do something to disappoint that colorful, cheerful bundle of sparkle and joy." I laugh at her description of Luna. "We've been planning the double baby shower for weeks now and I already baked cakes. I just needed to complain a bit and have you tell me how pretty I am."

God, she's so fucking perfect. How can every single thing she does make me love her even more?

"How about I *show* you how pretty you are? How beautiful and sexy and flawless I find you?"

"Do we have time?" She asks breathily, her pulse pounding in the side of her neck.

I nip at the spot and kiss away the sting. "We always have time for that, kitten." I don't give her time to answer, I just sink to my knees in front of her and spread her legs open for me.

She's wearing a pretty dress, one she bought just for the baby shower. I flip the skirt of the dress up and see she's not wearing any panties. I look up at her, over her baby bump, and she just shrugs, playing coy. I growl and pull her ass to the edge of the couch before attaching my mouth to her throbbing pussy.

"Yes!" She moans as I work my tongue in and out of her already soaking wet pussy. I suck on her folds and tease her clit, drinking down all of her sweetness.

Sienna grabs my hair and shoves me deeper into her cunt, making me chuckle. My baby wants it quick and dirty, and that's what she'll get. I roll her clit in between my lips and flick my tongue over it again and again while thrusting two fingers into her entrance and curling them up, hitting that spot that drives her crazy.

She rides my face and her thighs snap around my head, locking me in place. I grunt and double my efforts when I hear her gasping for air. Sucking on her clit, I lightly graze my teeth over the sensitive bundle of nerves and then swallow down her release as she gushes for me, coming to a shuddering climax at the tip of my tongue.

I clean up her pussy with long, languid laps of my tongue, smiling when she tugs me up by my hair, saying it's too much. It's not, but I'll let her have this out.

I smooth her dress back down and sit next to her, wrapping her up in my arms. "So, did we get that all cleared up?" I ask.

Sienna pops her cute little head up and smirks at me. "I might need another reminder in a few hours."

I open my mouth to respond, but a knock on the door cuts me off. I give Sienna a quick kiss and head towards the door, smirking to myself knowing that I'll have Sienna's taste in my mouth the entire shower.

Declan, Luna, and Asher file inside. Luna is a bright whirlwind of color as she makes her way over to Sienna. I'm so thankful the two of them have become such good friends. It makes me smile every time I think about our kids growing up together. I wonder how many children Declan and Luna want? Will Asher ever have kids?

I laugh to myself and shake my head. Not likely.

"What's got you smiling, brother?" Declan asks, thumping me on the back by way of greeting. Asher steps around us, nodding towards Sienna and heading towards the kitchen.

"Just wondering if Asher is ever going to have kids."

"Funny you should say that..."

"What?" I almost shout. "No way..."

"Calm down, it's nothing like that. I just think he might be seeing someone."

"Asher? Our brother? Asher Knight?"

"Yeah, smartass, Asher."

"What makes you say that?" I ask, still in denial. I mean, yeah, of course, I want the guy to meet someone and start a family. But I never thought it would actually happen.

"Just look at him," Declan answers.

I don't see anything out of the ordinary as I watch him grab a water bottle from the fridge and open it up. He leans back against the kitchen counter and looks at his watch, probably already bored and wishing he could leave.

"What am I looking for?"

"Wait for it..."

"Come on, Declan, are you messing with—"

"There! Look!"

I look over at Ash again and see him staring at his phone. Smiling. The dude is *smiling*. Grinning, actually, like a fool.

"Told you," Declan brags. "It happened while we were on the way over here too. He's *texting* and *smiling* and he doesn't seem nearly as insufferable as he usually is. Plus, have you noticed he's been traveling less?"

I didn't notice, but now that I think about it, he has been around the office more. Well, I'll be damned.

"What are you boys talking about over there?" Luna asks.

"Oh, nothing, hummingbird," Declan answers. It still gets me how much of a mushy sap he is around Luna. Sure, I'm a sap for Sienna too, but I always knew I had that capacity. Declan? Not so much. And Asher? Well, I can't wait to see how this will play out.

The baby shower comes and goes, guests file in and out, we play silly games and eat delicious food, and then Luna and Sienna sit on the couch with their feet propped up while Declan, Asher, and I clean up.

Once Sienna and I are alone again, I sit next to her on the couch and pull her into my lap.

"Cooper!" She squeals. "I'm too heavy!"

"Stop that, right now. You're perfect, and I already told you I love holding my whole family in my arms. Now be quiet and let me," I scold her, jokingly, of course.

She huffs out a little indignant breath. "So freaking bossy," she grumbles.

"Shh," I tease, tucking her head under my chin and rocking her back and forth.

"Mmm, you're good at this," she hums after a few moments. I grin at how easily I can get my kitten to calm down. "You're gonna be a good dad. Rocking our kids to sleep."

"I can't wait," I tell her truthfully.

"Me neither," she says, yawning and snuggling up closer to me.

"Get some rest, sweetness. I'll be right here when you wake up."

"I know," she responds, half asleep already. "You'll always be here."

Her words mean everything to me. I didn't think my heart could possibly contain any more joy or gratitude, but I suppose it will just have to grow a bit more to make some room. I drift off to sleep, holding my life, my love, my sweetness in my arms and rocking her gently.

"Love you, Cooper," she mumbles, sleepily.

"Love you more, sweetness."

Also by Cameron Hart

Check out my other popular series and books!
Mafia, MC, & Bodyguard Romance:
<u>Moscatelli Crime Family Series</u>[1]
<u>Di Salvo Crime Family Series</u>[2]
<u>Chaos MC series</u>[3]
<u>Savage Ride</u>[4]
Mountain Man Romance:
<u>Men of Blackthorne Mountain Series</u>[5]
<u>Bear's Tooth Mountain Men Series</u>[6]
Cowboy & Small Town Romance:
<u>Roped in by Love Series</u>[7]

---

1. https://books2read.com/u/mqBaze

2. https://books2read.com/u/m0odzW

3. https://books2read.com/u/bMVAOk

4. https://books2read.com/u/bMVlG7

5. https://books2read.com/u/3RYDvB

6. https://books2read.com/u/mVel7A

7. https://books2read.com/u/3RYlBY

About the Author

Hello. I'm Cameron Hart, and I write sweet steamy romances. I'm a *USA Today* Bestselling author with over forty books available. I write romance with lots of heat, plenty of sweet, and just enough drama to keep things interesting. I graduated from the Iowa Writer's Workshop in 2012 with a degree in creative writing. When I'm not working on my next book, I can be found reading, crocheting, doing yoga, and chasing around my grumpy cats.

What to expect from a Cameron Hart book: Lots of heat, plenty of sweet, and just enough drama to keep things interesting. No cheating, safe, guaranteed HEA!

Read more at https://cameronhart.net/.

9 798227 420749